W9-CQZ-515

'78 00354   days

THE KILLERS OF STARFISH

THE KILLERS

J. B. Lippincott Company

Philadelphia and New York

Jackson Gillis

OF STARFISH

*All characters in this book are fictional,
and any resemblance to persons living or dead is
purely coincidental.*

Copyright © 1977 by Jackson Clark Gillis
All rights reserved
First edition
9 8 7 6 5 4 3 2 1
Printed in the United States of America

U.S. Library of Congress Cataloging in Publication Data

Gillis, Jackson.
  The killers of Starfish.

  I. Title.
PZ4.G4826Ki [PS3557.I394]   813'.5'4   77-6231
ISBN-0-397-01201-2

to Patty, always . . .

1

It was the last ferry of the evening, and it sloshed toward the island through gathering veils of darkness and fog. Its customary cry of arrival, one long whistle followed by two shorts, echoed weakly against nearby rocks and dripping firs and the few ancient waterfront buildings of Whale Harbor.

In the coffee shop on the ferry's upper deck, a middle-aged man sipped from an empty cup. He was a shabby little man, even though his low-pulled hat and turned-up raincoat were brand new. But like his stiff, shiny shoes, they looked cheap and uncomfortable. The backs of his hands were sunburned. His nails were cracked and dirty. His face was buried in the Sunday sports section of the *Seattle Times*.

As the last blast of the ship's whistle faded back into the homelier clamor of complaining, tired kids and stacking dishes, the man finally raised his head to look at the bustle of activity around him. He had pale, watery eyes and his interest seemed only idly curious, but his glance took in every part of the room, every dripping window to the outside deck, every sweating face inside, every shivering face outside, every man and woman pulling on their coats, every bundled-up figure pushing toward the companion-way which led down toward the automobile deck.

Whatever he saw, or didn't see, apparently satisfied him and he put down his cup and newspaper. But his fingers were trembling, and he took a quick deep breath as he rose hurriedly to be one of the first to reach the stairway.

It was about thirty degrees colder on the auto deck, where an onshore wind was whistling the fog straight through its shadows, seemingly unhindered by the full load of assorted trucks and cars and campers. The man pulled his coat tighter, hesitating in momentary indecision: there were four rows of parked vehicles, two on each side of the companion-way structure; that meant six possible narrow lanes through which he could move. Which was safest, port or starboard?

"Forget where you parked, Clyde?"

A fat woman was eyeing him curiously. He stepped quickly out into the metal jungle without answering. His name wasn't Clyde and he didn't have a car. He moved toward the forward deck where a foot passenger could be the first to disembark. But the way was filled with obstructions, and there were more and more people pushing past him in the half darkness. The metal deck throbbed its steady engine rhythm —the ferry hadn't slowed down yet—but the man ducked his head and moved as fast as he could.

Somewhere out in the blackness straight ahead was the ferry's invisible target, the Whale Harbor ferry slip, a ramshackle combination of barnacled pilings and rotting timbers surrounded by the usual fish smells and sea gulls, though on a foul night like this one most of the gulls had the sense to stay huddled under the piers. And since this was the ferry's last trip, there was no friendly line of parked and lighted cars waiting up on the street behind the shed. There were only a couple of floodlights at the apex of the slip, where the heavy car ramp would soon drop down onto the ferry's deck. In the fog, those floodlights were about as useful as flashlights buried in feathers.

The oncoming ferry gave another blast of its whistle, its captain calmly listened to the pattern of the now-clearer echoes, and at just the right moment the ferry's engines were reversed to full speed astern.

The sudden heavy shaking of the deck almost made the man lose his footing. He steadied himself with one hand against the window of a station wagon. The window felt wet; the man realized that the wetness came from his own skin, his own sweat. Cold as it was down here, he was sweating.

There was a roar from inside the station wagon and a huge dog crashed against the glass beside his face. He stumbled back and banged his leg painfully against the high running board of a truck. It was a big diesel semi whose engine was just coughing into life. Other engines were starting up all around him. The auto deck was rapidly turning into a bedlam.

Meantime the ferry's port bow nuzzled with crushing force against pilings which sighed and creaked. Water churned white and waves raced along the rows of pilings as the starboard bow took its turn at trying to sink the pier on that side. But pilings and piers only swayed and groaned, first on one side and then the other, while ahead the first mooring hawser was dropped.

The man, nearing the forward deck, heard a car door slam close behind him. He glanced back, hesitating for one last second—then was blinded as headlights from an oil truck in the next lane snapped on and hit him full in the face. He turned ashen while more and more headlights flooded toward him, while more and more engines thundered into action.

In sudden panic he whirled to run past the last truck and onto the open deck. The big unloading ramp was in midair, being lowered, and a deckhand waiting beside the barrier cable caught at the man's arm, yelled at him to get back.

He ran toward the opposite railing. He was out of the direct rays of the truck lights there, and the busy deckhand didn't see him scramble up onto the railing —or, as the ferry swung close to that side once more, see him leap to grab for one of the rusty cables which bound the pilings together into "dolphins."

It wasn't a long jump and he got a good grip on the cable, even as the ferry's railing swung back out from under his feet. The tide was running high, so the heavy, less slippery timbers of the pier itself were not far to reach. Many a small boy had dreamed of trying this stunt and a few had perhaps accomplished it, though their punishment must have been horrible indeed, considering the peril involved.

But the shabby little man was apparently going to get away with it. He was scrambling up to grip a huge beam now, he was just about to disappear into the fog above . . . when for no visible reason he checked himself. He looked down with a startled blank look

10

on his white face, and then his grip on the beam relaxed. He slipped.

Hardly anyone saw him fall toward the narrowing gap of churning water below.

And over the roar of motors and horns, no one at all heard the awful scream as his body was crushed between ferry and pilings.

2

Jonas Duncan drove his blue pickup through the kaleidoscope of morning. On the right, Mrs. Kelly's late-blooming daffodils for the mainland markets. On the left, a mile of pink rhododendrons bursting into May. In the road straight ahead, nothing but a brown baby rabbit which Jonas swerved to miss.

He rounded the turn past Charlie's Woods and there was the water once more through the evergreens, stretching out toward another island and another and another. Today the sound was sparkling blue, though Jonas was learning that if you started to paint it that way it might suddenly turn to green or black. But never flat gray, not on a day when Mount Baker looked like a spilled quart of vanilla on the horizon, so close you could count the crevasses in the glaciers, if you had an eagle's eyesight. What was it, sixty miles away, maybe?

Oh, Jesus, if only he could paint it all like it felt, like it smelled, like it sparkled on a day like this! If only he could tell someone about it. If only she were beside him right now in the pickup so he could tell her—

He slammed on his brakes. A doe with two spotted fawns leaped off the road just in time, and he stopped remembering things as he yelled after the deer to boost them on their way. They faded silently into the dense undergrowth of ferns and Jonas Duncan grinned. He took a deep breath and yelled once more, just as loud and long as he could.

And then embarrassedly, hurriedly, Jonas put the pickup back into gear. There were probably enough people on the island already who suspected he was a damn fool. But as the pickup gained speed, he smiled again, quietly, and took another deep breath of spring. He hadn't coughed. He had yelled as loud as he could and he didn't even cough, not once!

Fifteen minutes later he was in the middle of town, parking the pickup in front of Davidson's Hardware and Building Supply, when he heard a shout from across the street. A portly man about Jonas's own age, clad in most of a deputy sheriff's uniform, was stepping hectically into the traffic, waving to Jonas and being well honked at because the only stoplight on the island was against him. Jonas recognized Bill Carruthers and waved him back, waited for the light to change, and then moved across to join him, laughing.

"Hey, do you get paid for giving yourself tickets?"

Bill only snorted. "Why the hell do we need a light, anyway?" He grabbed Jonas's arm to hustle him rapidly along the sidewalk.

"So more summer tourists will stop more often at more stores," Jonas answered, "so more taxes can be collected so more policemen—"

"Shut up," Bill muttered. "We got enough policemen already." He nodded ahead toward the modest entrance of Whale Harbor's modest hospital, where a young man with an impatient cigar in his mouth stood waiting for them. His hair was well tailored and his leisure suit casual, but the disguise was wasted. Even to Jonas's first glance, the modish smoker already looked more cop than Bill Carruthers could ever look.

"Captain Grayson. He's chief deputy, just flew over from the county seat half an hour ago," Bill said.

Grayson tossed his cigar into the gutter and interrupted Bill's introduction of Jonas. "Where've you been, Mr. Duncan? The sergeant here has been phoning all over, he tells me."

Jonas sighed, his sunlight fading. "You know anything about diesels? I thought I might find me a salmon this morning. But today it's a gasket, I think. This old boat I suckered for last fall, it likes to carry its oil in the bilge."

The voice was deep, easygoing, and Grayson looked directly at Jonas for the first time. He saw a shock of sandy hair—a weathered, big-featured face —an angular frame, clad in wool shirt and jeans, which made Jonas a little taller than Grayson was, even in his new high-heeled cowboy boots. But quite a few people were taller than Grayson, and he quickly noted that although there wasn't much extra padding over Jonas's belt, the sandy hair was well salted with gray and there were more than sunburn wrinkles around the quiet eyes. Jonas's worn logging boots were caked with dried mud and he apparently hadn't shaved yet this morning. Maybe Jonas was nothing but another aging Californian going native, going to seed. Maybe he wouldn't be any trouble

14

after all. Grayson gave him an innocent smile. "Had your breakfast yet?" he asked.

Jonas didn't answer the smile. He nodded toward the hospital. "Why, you got a corpse in there you want me to look at?"

Bill Carruthers started to cough but Grayson was already striding toward the hospital entrance to lead them inside. As they moved through the small receiving office and along a corridor, the chief deputy spoke coldly over his shoulder. "Who told you, Duncan?"

"You, captain. Pretty obvious, isn't it?"

"Well, it's all over the island," Bill Carruthers interceded, "about that guy getting squashed by the ferry last night. Only when it comes to finding anybody who really saw it happen—"

"This is my bit, sergeant," said Grayson. "Do you mind?"

As they followed him through a green door, Jonas gave Bill Carruthers a curious look but the local deputy only shrugged. They were in the hospital's one operating room, now pinch-hitting as an autopsy room, and it was crowded. To one side a couple of men were poking at a small pile of clothing. Another man, part of a group around the operating table farther on, was taking pictures. One of the doctors present was Dan Sturdevant, whose hospital this was, and Dan didn't look too happy with the invasion. There was no one else here whom Jonas could recognize. Apparently Captain Grayson had flown in this morning with a full crew. Why?

While Grayson moved on to mutter to another doctor, a county medical examiner probably, Jonas paused to look more closely at the pile of clothing and cheap pocket items which were being spread out for fingerprinting. Then Grayson called to him and the others stepped back a little from the operating table to make room.

"The body's over here, Duncan."

Jonas moved closer, taking his time. He looked down at the sprawled naked thing on the table. The doctors hadn't done much to it, yet. But Bill Carruthers was correct; the poor guy had been squashed, all right.

His head was only cut and bruised, however. And Jonas looked expressionlessly at the dead face for a long moment before he finally shrugged.

"You're out of luck, captain. I never saw this guy before." Jonas grinned. "Sorry if that disappoints you."

Grayson frowned. "Take another look."

"After seventeen years of lineups I don't need another look."

"You sure? You positive you never saw him before?"

Grayson had been rubbing him the wrong way ever since they first saw each other, and probably on purpose, Jonas knew. But the hell with it. Jonas didn't enjoy corpses at any time of day. "Just as sure as I am that you don't need me to tell you who this is," Jonas said coldly. "It's written all over him. He just got out of prison, right? The easiest identification in the world."

"Did Sergeant Carruthers tell you—?"

Jonas gestured to where the fingerprint man and others were working. "Before the water made such a mess of it, that stuff was brand new. And the labels are all from the same store—in Walla Walla. Besides, where else can a man get a haircut like that any more? Or an amateur tattoo? Only he's been out in the sun, so maybe he was a trusty there and worked outdoors."

Grayson was already taking Jonas's arm to lead him off to one side. "Okay, you're a lot faster than our men were last night."

"I can afford to guess, they can't."

"Now don't be sore."

"I'm not sore."

Grayson put a piece of paper in Jonas's hand. "Here. His name was Wilbur Styles. He just got out of the state penitentiary after four years and three months with good behavior."

"Didn't do him much good," Jonas said, not looking at the paper. "Captain, all I want to know is what *I'm* doing here. Why you thought I'd even be interested in Styles."

"He was arrested in Los Angeles once. After all your experience with the LAPD—"

"On what charge?"

"Well, bunco, I'll admit—"

"And I was Homicide. Like you are sometimes, right?" Jonas gestured to the room. "Isn't that what this is all about? You've suddenly decided Mr. Styles was murdered, maybe? Like someone *pushed* him off that ferry, maybe?"

"No," Grayson said, "he wasn't pushed."

He fished in his pocket and produced a small envelope. He opened the envelope. Inside it was a little lump of metal.

"This hit him," he said. "This is what made him fall."

Jonas touched the little slug, rolled it between his fingers. "Pretty small. What is it, twenty-five caliber?"

Grayson nodded. "Your local doctor there spotted it this morning, started probing. It was almost entirely embedded in Styles's spine."

Jonas put the slug back in the envelope and lifted the piece of paper in his hand. It was a Xerox of the victim's record. While Jonas looked at it, Grayson expanded.

"And of course nobody heard a gun fired, not in all the noise, cars and everything. At least nobody we've talked to yet. And there were at least a hundred people on that ferry, plus the crew, going by ticket sale records, but they're never exactly right. So far, we've identified and talked to maybe thirty-five locals who were aboard, including kids. None of them saw one damn thing that helps."

Jonas handed the piece of paper back to Grayson. "You've got your work cut out for you. I'm no help, either."

"There's nothing on his record there . . . ?"

Jonas shook his head sympathetically. Maybe Grayson was human after all. "No bells. I'm sorry. They retired me nearly six years ago. When you're out of the business you lose touch."

As they moved out of the room together, Grayson's voice was friendly. "Yes, they handed you an early medical, I understand. Look pretty healthy now, though."

Jonas glanced quickly at him.

"But you didn't really quit, did you? Worked for a

18

couple of years as a private investigator in Santa Monica, isn't that so?"

"Part time," Jonas said. "I didn't like it."

"And up here I've heard your name in connection with a couple of things."

"I'm retired," Jonas said firmly. "I paint a few pictures, do a little fishing, that's all. Right now I've got to buy a new gasket. See you."

He started down the corridor but Grayson stayed with him. Grayson was smiling his innocent smile again. "You'll let me know if anything occurs to you, anything at all?"

"It won't."

"It might. See, that dead guy you never heard of in there had a slip of paper in his pocket with your name and telephone number on it."

Jonas stopped abruptly. He stared at Grayson. "I was beginning to think you only wore one shoe," he finally said. "So that's why you've been checking up on me. Whose handwriting?"

"His own, probably. No, I'd already heard how you interfered in that case over in Skagit County at Christmastime—"

"I helped somebody, that's all. For only a day or two. It was a manslaughter case; they'd arrested the wrong person."

"Sure, and a friend of mine got demoted for it. So let's not either one of *us* make any mistakes, okay? And now I'll try again. Because if you didn't know Styles, like you're so very sure, then how come your name and telephone number—"

"I told you, captain, I'm retired."

Jonas walked out.

3 "Just a nothing, huh? Guy wasn't anybody at all." Charlie spoke softly, absently. He was chipping on the nose of a bear and he didn't want to split it. "Piece of sand in the desert. Spit in the ocean."

"He was a con man, a paperhanger," said Jonas, "a three-time loser."

"My wife wrote a bad check in Tacoma once."

"Charlie, I thought you might remember a little more about that phone call you mentioned last night. You said it was a man. What else?"

"I'm trying."

They were in the abandoned garage on E Street which Charlie called his downtown studio. Charlie was getting ready for the summer tourist trade, and the floor was littered with shavings and dried logs of various sizes. Charlie Tlulagit was a Haida Indian with five kids to support.

Jonas opened a can of beer and passed it to Charlie and waited. "You did a nice job patching my roof," Jonas said. "Thanks."

"Sure. Only now your ceiling needs a little repainting. Hey, you suppose that's how Michelangelo got

20

started? 'Pope,' he said, 'as long as I'm up here on this ladder—' "

"Charlie."

"Well, it was five thirty in the afternoon. I was just about to pack up my tools when I heard your phone ringing. A man said, 'Is this Mr. Duncan? Mr. Jonas Duncan?' And I said sorry, but you'd gone over to the other side of the island for dinner and navigation night school—which you sure need—and you probably wouldn't be home until maybe nine thirty or ten. Then he said something else only I couldn't hear what it was, so I said what was that? But I couldn't hear his answer, either, so I said well if you'll talk louder and give me your name and number—only then he hung up."

"But *how* did he sound, Charlie? If he wouldn't leave his name he might have been scared to, or maybe he was mad or at least in a hurry."

"Why? Maybe he just had to pee. Anyway, all I could hear was this panting and a sort of pounding in my ears—"

"A what?"

"From me! I'd just climbed off your damned roof!" Charlie took a drink, handed the beer can back, and looked curiously at Jonas's frown. "So maybe it was this guy Styles and maybe it wasn't. What's the difference? They bugging you about it?"

"I didn't mention that phone call to the police."

"Why should you? It could have been anybody. Or nobody."

"I just told them I'd never heard of Styles. Only the trouble is, suppose he *was* the one who called. You told him I'd be home later. So suppose that's why he

21

was on the ferry. Suppose he was on his way to see me."

"So he was in such a hurry he got this crazy idea he'd be a sea gull? Jonas, that cat must have been running away from something, not toward it!"

"Like a gun. I know. But whoever shot him at a time like that took an awful chance. Somebody was awfully anxious to stop him."

"Stop him from what? Just from coming to see you? Don't be such an egotist. I can think of ten other explanations."

"So can I," said Jonas. "But I keep thinking of that one. I'd be sorry if it was that one."

Charlie lowered his chisel and looked at the older man, who sometimes didn't seem older at all. "You must have been a lousy cop," Charlie said.

Jonas didn't answer for a moment. He took a thoughtful drink from the beer can. "Maybe," he said. "Maybe I was."

"Oh, for Christ's sake!"

"I know," Jonas said quickly, "it's their murder, not mine. Somebody who was following Styles on that ferry shot him, and he fell and was crushed to death. Only nobody saw anything. Nobody ever does. I wouldn't want the job."

"That's better! I mean, just because the creep had your name in his pocket—"

"I was the arresting officer."

"Huh?"

Jonas took a deep breath. "After I left the hospital, I stopped by at the phone company, to call LA. A friend of mine in the file section down there says they've been digging their whole record on Wilbur

Styles. He was picked up there only once, for trying to raffle off a used car he didn't own; the charges were dropped after a preliminary hearing. But my number was on it. Charlie, I was the one who arrested him."

"Oh!" Charlie reached quietly for the beer.

"I didn't remember him," Jonas went on unhappily. "Nothing about him. Not his face, not his name —and the hell of it is, I *still* don't remember!"

"He couldn't have been much. It couldn't have been very important."

"I must have just blocked. Grayson had been rubbing me the wrong way. But that's no damned excuse—"

Charlie suddenly interrupted. "Hey, when was this? When did you pick Styles up?"

Jonas hesitated. "Well, he was younger then, probably looked a little different. It was twenty-one years ago."

Charlie burst into laughter. "Is that all? Oh, you're losing your marbles! Let's see, a cop arrests maybe three people a day, that's like fifteen a week, times fifty is seven or eight hundred a year, times how many years?"

Jonas took the beer out of Charlie's hand and finished it while Charlie went happily back to work on the bear.

"The trouble with you, Jonas, is you just haven't got the hang of living on an island yet. Up here, you're not supposed to worry about anything any more. Ever. Not about anything or anybody anywhere but right here."

Jonas put the empty can down and rose. "Sure," he

said. "The rest of the world are just suckers to sell phony totem poles to." He moved to the open door to look out to the street.

"Sit down," Charlie said. "There is no such thing as a phony totem pole."

"Oh, hell," Jonas said. "Here comes Bill Carruthers again."

"A totem pole is for telling a story. About people, about a family. Start reading from the top. It can be any size you want, any color, stick it on your lawn or up on the roof if you feel that big—"

"What happened to your wife in Tacoma?" Jonas interrupted, stepping back from the doorway.

"The bad check? Oh, she'd put the wrong book in her purse; it was just an accident, that's all. But you think anybody'd listen to her? To an Indian? To a pregnant Indian?"

"So she was a nothing, too," Jonas said, "a nobody." He moved toward the alley with quick decision.

"Hey, what'll I not say? Where didn't you go?"

"Walla Walla."

4 She lived in the old part of town, the part that wasn't trying to imitate the San Fernando Valley. She lived in the upstairs of a big garage that might have been a carriage house once, or more likely a one-cow-and-pony barn. There was green grass sprouting all around the garage, even on the driveway, and fruit trees were in blossom any way you looked. Spring came later here east of the mountains than it did on Jonas's island, so the colors were all starting to splash at once.

Jonas walked along the driveway past a white-painted gingerbread house which was apparently a student rooming house and maybe had been one for the past half century; the nearby college was at least twice that old. Everything in this quiet part of Walla Walla seemed old and Victorian but clean and prosperous at the same time. It looked like some places in New England looked once and didn't, any more. Jonas climbed the outside stairway of the garage and rang a door chime made out of colored pieces of cheap glass.

The woman who opened the door was plump and nearsighted. She wore a rumpled white uniform and

25

the badge of a nurse's aide. Her white stockings had slipped into tired creases and balloons around her ankles. Her touched-up hair needed another touch-up.

"Mrs. Styles? Mrs. Wilbur Styles?"

She peered sharply at him, then nodded into a handkerchief, and Jonas realized that she had been crying and he suddenly felt guilty for noticing her ankles. She gestured for him to step inside before he had even said who he was or why he was here. He told her his name, then, but she only nodded as though she didn't care or already knew and dabbed at her nose with her flowered wet hanky as she waved him past a table laden with porcelain puppies and kittens toward her even more cluttered living room.

There was another visitor there, squeezed between the narrow arms of a flower-printed chair. He was a local parole officer who had come to pay a sympathy call, and he looked uncomfortable, for sympathy seemed to make Mrs. Styles cry. He struggled awkwardly to his feet to pump Jonas's hand, while a parakeet in a pink cage screamed at both of them. The man was just about to go, he was relieved to announce, but he was sure glad to meet anybody from LA. His wife had a sister in Orange County and, besides, the man had been hearing Jonas's name mentioned, but this was no time to gab. Obviously what the man wanted most was to get away from reminiscing about a dead ex-con with his dowdy widow. The woman was a spigot.

"Who mentioned my name?" Jonas tried to make it as casual as he could. "One of the boys over at the prison?"

"Well, yes, I understand you were over there asking a few questions this afternoon."

Small towns, Jonas thought, they're all alike. He said, "I used to know one of the assistant wardens. He did some graduate work once at UCLA."

"Mort Crowley, sure. But of course the police have been around, too. Talking to me and Mrs. Styles here, both."

"That so?"

"At the request of somebody named Grayson, I understand. He seems to be right on the ball. Phoned with all sorts of questions about poor Wilbur. But Grayson, he's the one who actually mentioned your name. He said you might come visiting. Said you were okay."

"That was nice of him." Jonas nodded, wondering why he'd been in such a hurry to get here. He didn't think Mort Crowley would have advertised his presence. But he might have known Grayson would discover he had left home and so send out signals, just in case.

"Well, I stayed too long already," the parole officer was saying as he edged toward the door. "Just remember, Dora, if there's anything I can do . . ."

While Mrs. Styles squeezed the man's hands in wet gratitude, Jonas smiled. "You must be a good parole officer," Jonas said. "You seem to have known her husband pretty well, and yet he'd only been out of prison a couple of weeks."

"Oh, Wilbur was one of my charges five years ago, too," the man answered. "His last time around. That was for cashing some phony bonds over in Pasco."

"It was my birthday." Mrs. Styles sniffled. "But do you think the judge would listen? I remember Wilbur had just come back from Portland. He knew how much I wanted a color television, only this job fell through and he didn't want to tell me; he knew how much I love birthdays."

The parole officer mumbled hastily, "Yes, well, it's been nice to meet you, Mr. Duncan. And if there's anything she can't tell you about that slip of paper, or about anything I told Wilbur—"

Jonas moved after him. "About what? Wait a minute."

Mrs. Styles was opening the door for the man and she shrugged through her tears to Jonas. "That slip of paper they say was in Wilbur's pocket with your name on it, that's all. It's not important."

"Well, I couldn't help but be curious," Jonas said.

The parole officer turned briskly on the little porch outside. "Don't blame you. But somebody at the prison mentioned your name to him just before he was discharged, Wilbur told me."

"Yes, that was Mort Crowley, I find. He just hadn't had a chance to write to me about it yet."

"Well, I gave Wilbur several names, too. It's like giving names to an alcoholic. People he can look up in case he's ever in your neck of the woods and needs help."

"I understand."

"Wilbur went to Seattle to look for employment," Mrs. Styles said righteously.

The parole officer nodded. "Yes, I gave Wilbur permission to go over to the Puget Sound area several days ago. He had the idea he might be a fisherman again—that's what he was once—or a salesman, maybe. I explained all that to the police."

"It's what he was before I met him, years ago." The

28

pathetic tremor was in Mrs. Styles's voice again. "A commercial fisherman, back before the bottom dropped out."

"Anyway," the parole officer concluded, "I told Wilbur in no uncertain terms to stay out of trouble. And if he felt the itch to write a check or anything, to go talk it over with somebody first, somebody who didn't wear a badge but who knew the ropes, like yourself. Especially you, since Wilbur seemed to remember your name from somewhere. So I'm afraid I'm the one who told Wilbur to look up your number and keep it in his pocket. Sorry if it's caused you any trouble."

So that was it. That's all there was to it. And apparently everyone in Walla Walla knew about it, knew about everything. Jonas suddenly felt tired. What the hell had he expected? Why did he fly over here in the first place? He heard Mrs. Styles blowing her nose and he turned to her.

"Maybe I'd better leave now, too," he said.

"But I haven't eaten!" she gasped. She looked Jonas straight in the eye and she sounded quite offended. "When you called from the prison and asked me if I'd like to go out for dinner, I just skipped eating for the rest of the day! And I worked all last night and there's been police and neighbors here practically every minute since this morning. . . . Oh, dear"—tears were flooding her eyes again, apologetic ones this time—"I'm sorry, you do what you like; it's an imposition, I know." She stopped. Jonas let her wait for a minute before answering.

"No, it's not," he said quietly. "Why don't we go right now? I'll wait for you outside."

She nodded and Jonas thought he caught a tiny

smug look in her eyes as she shut the door. He turned to trot down the stairway after the parole officer.

They stopped on the grass below. The parole officer grinned. "Looks like you're stuck, friend. Can't say I envy you. Oh, not that I blame the poor gal for taking it so hard," he added quickly, "she's a decent woman, well respected here."

"Sure." Jonas shrugged. "When I heard Wilbur Styles had a wife right here in town, I thought I'd better give her a call. Only I wanted to ask you, was there anything else you didn't say in there? Mort told me when he mentioned my name to Styles it seemed to hit some kind of chord, but Styles wouldn't explain; he wasn't much for talking to wardens, apparently."

The parole officer grinned and gestured toward the upstairs apartment. "I didn't want to dig you in any deeper with her. But you know what Wilbur told me once? If he ever had to be arrested again, he'd go back and do it in Los Angeles, because that's where the first decent cop he ever met was. He'd always remembered you, Mr. Duncan."

"Jesus!" Jonas said. "Do you know I still can't even remember—"

The parole officer interrupted with an understanding laugh. "Oh, hell, why would you? It doesn't mean anything, neither did he. Forget it! Happens all the time!"

"Wait a minute," Jonas said. "Do you have any idea who might have murdered him? He hadn't made any enemies in prison, apparently."

"Or anywhere else, that I know of. Wilbur never got mixed up in anything that important. I hate to say this, but he just wasn't the kind you'd think was worth killing!"

The parole officer departed with a friendly wave. A few moments later, Mrs. Styles came hurrying out with a well-worn coat over her uniform and a scarf of clashing color tied over her hair. As she came down the stairway, Jonas saw that she had repaired her face a bit and there wasn't a trace of those crocodile tears any more.

"Okay," he said, "what's this all about? I didn't phone you."

She looked him straight in the eye again. "But you came here, didn't you? Let's go," she said. "I'm so hungry I could eat a goddamn horse."

5 The place she wanted to go to was in the new part of town, on the highway. It was made of plastic and neon and it specialized in lobster steaks, cheese dressings, and live country-western music. It could have been in Texas, Massachusetts, or Michigan, and it was exactly the sort of place where Dora would like to be seen dining with a handsome stranger. Not that Jonas fully qualified for that description—he was rather careless about his hair, which could stand a cutting, Dora noticed, and his tweed jacket looked a bit rumpled for her taste. But he had eyes that could intimidate a waiter when necessary and he wasn't at all awkward in the way he pulled her chair out for her when they sat down. Certainly no one would ever suspect he was nothing but an ex-cop, though Dora did understand that he had been a lieutenant once. On the other hand, he was much too rough-cut and outdoors-looking to be taken for a distinguished banker or attorney. Perhaps people would think he was in timber, or dam construction, or maybe he was a big wheat rancher: yes, that would be nice.

From Jonas's view, between splatters of ketchup

and applause for the noisy singers in spangled jeans, the place and the company looked more ordinary. It wasn't surprising to him that Dora would have taken advantage of his presence here to get an evening out, particularly after the shock of her husband's death. It was quite natural that she might want to let her hair down in front of an out-of-towner with whom she could safely drink too much and even comfortably say shit if she felt like it. Jonas tried to feel honored. But it wasn't easy. Because he soon began to think that the main reason Dora had invented that telephoned invitation of his, the main reason she hadn't simply asked him to stay on in her house after the parole officer's departure, so she could say whatever she had to say right then, was plain old paranoia. Dora had been questioned today by several different policemen, from friendly locals to one of Captain Grayson's own assistants who had flown in with photos of the body and of Wilbur's clothing and possessions (Dora had picked out those nice decent clothes for Wilbur herself, she said; Wilbur had no more taste than a hippie). And any one of those policemen, she claimed, could easily have planted a bug in her little apartment. Dora had worked in public hospitals as a nurse, or almost one, for many years, and she knew only too well what cops on a murder case were like. They had no scruples at all. Why, any one of them could have slipped one of those tiny listening devices into one of her precious toy animals, perhaps—oh, the bastards, the dirty bastards, to take advantage of the things closest to a poor widow's heart! But when Jonas quickly asked why, why the police would be so interested in what she might say,

Dora changed the subject and glanced cautiously toward a nearby table where there was no one but an early-dining couple with their noisy kids.

And when Jonas asked what she wanted to tell him that was so important and secret, Dora was evasive again. Three men in business suits had just come in, and they sat down not far away. They were young, tanned, confident-looking men, and it took Jonas several minutes to convince Dora that the police simply never tail people in groups of three. Besides, who could eavesdrop over those steel guitars? Jonas smiled and suggested that the three men were probably nothing more dangerous than engineers or scientists from the Hanford Project, plotting the disposal of a few thousand tons of atomic waste. But his effort at lightness drew only a blank look. "Of what?" Dora asked, and Jonas didn't repeat it. She seemed incapable of recognizing a joke, and Jonas felt foolish for trying so hard.

She talked willingly and bluntly about Wilbur, but Jonas learned little that he couldn't already guess. The Styleses had been married for about ten years. Six of those years Wilbur had spent loafing in prison. All of them Dora had spent working her fingers to the bone. They met in San Francisco, at a time when she had a job in a drug-control center in Haight-Ashbury and Wilbur was discovering that there were even fewer fishing boats still working out of the bay than there were salmon trawlers left in Seattle. He worked occasionally as a weekend crewman on private sailing boats and talked grandly of maybe crewing in the Honolulu yacht race someday, but of course it never happened. Wilbur was nothing but a

34

dreamer and Dora knew it. But he always said nice things about her cooking. He could make her laugh and he said she was pretty when she knew damn well she wasn't. He told funny stories about how he pretended he was a street preacher once and people put pennies and dimes in his hat to save the sinners in Hollywood. He showed her how he looked as a process server, scaring a lovelorn girl off a guy's back with phony child-support claims from the guy's two nonexistent wives. Oh, yes, Wilbur had his devilish side, all right. But he only did things like that for fun and she didn't really believe they were true, anyway. Besides, he always brought her gifts, like nobody had ever done before—flowers or candy or more expensive things—until she said maybe she'd just have to marry him to make him save his money for the really nice furnishings she'd always dreamed of having in a nest, a home of her own. Wilbur picked up the cue and proposed, and it wasn't until Dora was proudly wearing a genuine 18-carat gold wedding band that she discovered how Wilbur had *really* raised that extra money he'd been spending on her: by forging drug prescriptions for addicts.

Dora saw the twitch in Jonas's eye, and she hastily insisted that Wilbur never did such an awful thing again in his whole life. Oh, no, Dora saw to that, and there was no more crap about being a seasonal fisherman or sailor, either. She hauled Wilbur back to Washington, where he got occasional safe work like picking fruit or selling used cars. Then, after his second conviction, he was sent to Walla Walla and she moved there to be closer for the Sunday visits, which she never missed. And during the times when Wilbur *was* out of prison, except for a couple of quick escapes to look at the sea, they were as happy and respectable as honeymooners, she said. If only poor Wilbur hadn't had that fatal weakness in his character which at periodic intervals let the devil in. Oh, but never again farther than to lure Wilbur into passing a bad check or cashing a phony stock certificate at Christmas or helping a friend feed his hungry family with a phony insurance claim, by forging a few harmless affidavits, maybe. "I mean, nothing ever again that could have hurt real people instead of just supermarkets or banks," Dora said firmly.

Jonas listened as patiently as he could. It was something he owed, maybe, to listen. When Jonas was a very young policeman he was assigned to Traffic Detail and often, far too often, he and his partner would have to knock on some strange door and ask if this was where so-and-so lived. And when the startled occupant said yes, then the trick was to say it all as quickly as you could, say something about regretting to inform you, ma'am, or sir, without once really remembering that it was a human being you had just seen spread across an intersection or burning up under a truck. Yes, say it quick and get out of there fast. Hide behind your uniform and, above all, don't let yourself listen.

But by the time Dora Styles was through with San Francisco and into her second piece of apple pie, Jonas had about decided that Dora simply didn't have anything much to say about her husband's death. Maybe she only wanted to prolong this evening, prolong this day. Wilbur had never been anything in life, so maybe he would be in death. Maybe she could still *make* him into something. At any rate, this was Dora's moment of attention and she didn't want it to end. And as for paranoia, what better security blanket is there? Only important people get bugged.

It wasn't until he finally got her out of there and into his rental car in the cold parking lot that Dora mentioned the telephone call from Wilbur. It had happened just two days before his death, and he was calling from somewhere around Seattle, she thought. Anyway, Wilbur had reversed the charges, and the reason he phoned was to tell Dora that he might be staying a few days longer than he had planned because he had just located someone who might give him a job, someone he'd discovered quite by accident through one of the names on his list.

List? What list? Dora fumbled surreptitiously in her purse and pulled out a piece of paper on which she had scribbled some names. Wilbur's own list, unfortunately, was mostly in his head. But these were the names he had mentioned, the places where he was going to look for work, and Dora had written them all down, every single one that she could remember.

Jonas peered curiously at the list in the feeble glow of his dash light. "Harry at the cannery," he read. "Mr. Campbell, friend of the warden's." The name of a used-car man, an employment agency. "Jody's Sport Fishing Pier, see Jody himself."

Jonas snapped off the light without finishing the list. He realized that Dora was staring tautly at him now.

"Okay," he said, "go on."

"Go on?"

"When he called you, what else did he say?"

"Well, that's all. But he did sound like his old happy self, like way back before we were married."

"That's all?" It was hard for Jonas to keep irritation out of his voice. "Mrs. Styles, don't you realize the police already know most of this? Or *some* officials do. They're the ones who gave your husband most of these names in the first place."

"I know," she said.

"And the ones they didn't give him I'll have to tell them about, sooner or later."

"All right."

"You really should have told the police yourself."

"They won't do anything. You know that."

"It seems to me they've been pretty busy already."

"Oh, sure," she said tartly. "Busy sweeping it under the rug. Maybe they'll even decide Wilbur stole something and was running away—or he cheated somebody, or he sold them some drugs—but it was all his fault, of course, he was nothing but an ex-con, so why bother with who killed him? Just work real quick to find the simplest answer there is and forget it! He deserved what he got, so forget him!"

"Mrs. Styles, what makes you think I could do any better? What makes you think I'd even want to?"

"You're here, aren't you?" Her voice was beginning to tremble.

"But how can I help if all you've got to go on—"

"Wilbur sounded excited and happy," she interrupted. "He'd just talked to somebody on the telephone, somebody he thought could really help him."

"Somebody? Didn't he say who it was?"

"No, I don't even remember if he said 'him' or 'her.'"

"But didn't you ask him?"

"No."

"Didn't he say *anything* more than that?"

"No!" she wailed. "I wouldn't let him, don't you understand? He'd been talking more than three minutes already, it was long-distance collect, so I made him hang up!"

Jonas almost laughed, he couldn't help himself.

Dora's pleading eyes flashed with anger. "So the only name in his pocket was yours, so for some damn reason he always remembered your name, what good did *you* do him?" she said.

"I'm sorry, Mrs. Styles," he said gently. "But I live on an island and he just never got there, and—"

She burst into sudden, hysterical laughter. "Oh, can you ever say *that* again! My dumb damn husband, he just never got there in his whole damn life!"

And then she started to cry, exhaustedly, helplessly. Jonas quietly slipped her list into his pocket. These tears were real.

6 At the seventh name on the list he hit pay dirt.

The name was Brighton Walker, Inc., and it was etched in gold on double mahogany doors, along with the even more impressive words in silver (or maybe it was platinum), *Development Design.* Jonas took one look and almost turned back to the elevators. He might have, if it hadn't been raining outside and his city raincoat needed drying out. The next time he came to Seattle he'd bring his old oilskin and the devil with how it smelled. Anyway, this was about the last place on earth where Wilbur Styles might have come looking for work—which only made it that much more intriguing, so Jonas sighed and went through the heavenly gates.

Half an hour later he found himself the sole remaining occupant of a revolving-door reception room which had been borrowed from a Beverly Hills art gallery. The velvet walls were covered with paintings, mostly paintings of buildings, like a couple of well-framed and lighted and signed Utrillos which Jonas thought damn near had to be real. Some other oils were even more expensively mounted and displayed but the buildings weren't in Paris, they were in places called Leisure Village and Cascade Estates and Chateau Condominia, which all looked exactly the same. Mr. Brighton Walker, it seemed, was a real estate promoter. But when Jonas reacted to that discovery (he had expected a designer at least, an architect or builder), then the young male receptionist quickly put Jonas back in his place with "He's the one who conceived this very building, you know."

"I'll be damned," Jonas said, and he turned to look out the huge picture window for the tenth time. He could still see nothing but gray scudding clouds where Elliott Bay should be. Off to the right he caught a brief glimpse of the Space Needle restaurant. From here it seemed to float in and out of view like a shy flying saucer. And down, thirty stories straight down, there were occasional silent flashes of toy cars on the wet streets. Well, it was a pretty impressive building, all right, and Brighton Walker was no doubt very important. And the odds were a hundred to one that he simply wasn't the right Brighton Walker, wasn't the same Brighton Walker whose name Wilbur Styles had mentioned to Dora. Jonas glanced at his watch. His raincoat was about dry, now.

"Sorry your having to wait so long. It's really best to make an appointment," said the receptionist between phone calls. The young man's name was Terrence Fall and he seemed pretty straight, despite occasional traces of a Boston accent which sounded like something he'd learned in dramatic school.

"That's okay," said Jonas.

"You sure there's nothing I can do? I'm not just the

41

receptionist, you know. She's having a baby. What I mean is, ordinarily I'm one of Mr. Walker's special assistants."

"Learning the trade, eh?" Jonas nodded. "The real estate dodge."

Terrence grinned, relaxing a bit. "Yeah," he said, "you guessed it. I just got my license." A phone rang again. Apparently it wasn't anyone important, for Terrence shunted the caller into next week with the coldness of a traffic cop. Others he would put through to Mr. Walker with the deference of a royal butler. "I thought of being a TV announcer," he said, "but they expect you to learn all that journalism."

"I'm sure you'll do just fine here," said Jonas. "And thanks, but I don't mind waiting. I only want to ask Mr. Walker a question or two, that's all. It might be personal."

"Oh," Terrence said, looking at Jonas a bit more curiously.

Mostly just to change the subject, Jonas tapped a framed photograph on the wall beside him. It was a photograph of a thirty- or forty-foot sailing boat, a ketch. "This one of your boss's yachts?"

Terrence smiled. "Hey, he's not that rich. Oh, Mr. Walker has a boat, all right, but just one. It's a big cabin cruiser. Anyway, that's an old picture. That's the boat Trevor Vance sailed around the world in."

Jonas shrugged. "Tough life," he said. The name Trevor Vance meant nothing to him.

"He's the man who owns Starfish Island," Terrence explained, with a touch of professional pride. "We're putting a deal together there."

Jonas's heart skipped a beat. He turned back for another look at the photograph of the sailboat. There was a bridge in the background, he now noticed, which looked like the Golden Gate Bridge. "Deal?" he said casually.

"You know. Development concept, environmental study, the whole ball of planning wax, everything for complete waterfront living."

Jonas ignored the lingo. "Sure is a beautiful boat," he said enviously. "Only me, I could never afford the crew it would take, or the moorage fees."

"Crew? Oh, I guess he was human and picked up a girl now and then, but most of the trip he was all alone. That picture was taken ten or twelve years ago, right after he got back."

"Alone!" Jonas seized on it. "Imagine handling a big boat like that all alone. I'd like to meet that man."

Terrence seemed a bit startled by Jonas's interest. "Well, I'm not sure," Terrence said. "You understand Starfish is still on the drawing board, so what I just said is sort of confidential."

"Oh, I don't care about real estate," Jonas said. "But I've got a boat myself, you understand? And I go out alone on it, sometimes. And I've always wanted to talk to somebody who had the guts to go all the way around the world by himself. What's this Trevor Vance's phone number, over there on Starfish?"

Jonas paused. Terrence was looking at him even more strangely.

"What's the matter?" Jonas asked. "I wouldn't really bother him."

"No, no, it's just funny, that's all," Terrence said. "You're the second person who's looked at that picture and started asking questions."

"I am? Who was the other discerning yachtsman?"

43

Terrence laughed. "I wouldn't exactly describe him that way. He was kind of a shabby little guy. Came in here last Friday. I think he was just looking for a handout, only Mr. Walker was up in Vancouver anyway, and the guy started to leave. But then he spotted that same picture from clear across the room and started asking questions, so I told him about Mr. Vance, same as I told you. Of course, I'm no buddy of Vance's like Mr. Walker is, but I've been out there to Starfish Island a couple of times—"

It was Terrence who stopped talking this time, so abruptly he almost choked. Jonas couldn't blame him. Because the woman who had just walked into the office was easily one of the most beautiful women Jonas had ever seen. She wasn't young and she was long and lanky, but when she moved everything moved in the right place at the right time. She had clear pale skin, brown hair, and startling emerald eyes which looked straight through Jonas and didn't even see him. Or didn't deign to, maybe. She had to be a princess at least. Right now she was the Snow Queen. While Terrence turned red and noticed that the phone on his desk was ringing again, she pulled off her little rain hat. The drops of water on it sparkled like icicles.

"Excuse me," Terrence mumbled, bumping his elbow as he grabbed for his telephone.

The woman daintily shook her icicles onto Terrence's desk. "No," she said, "and don't answer that." Her voice was low-pitched and precise, like a fortune teller's or an executioner's.

"I'm sorry," Terrence said, dropping his phone in the wrong place.

44

"Is Brighton in? I'm in a hurry."

"Well, he's talking to Florida, I think. He asked not to be disturbed for a few minutes."

"Isn't that too bad about Florida," she said sweetly, and she dropped her wet umbrella onto Terrence's in-basket and strode toward the private offices. As she moved she gave Jonas a veiled, curious glance which she didn't think would be noticed. But it was. Lots of women are beautiful when angry, Jonas thought. But some are beautiful when frightened, too. It was startling to realize that this woman just might be both.

The moment she was gone, Terrence jerked the umbrella off his basket and threw it onto the carpet.

Jonas spoke quietly. *"Mrs.* Brighton Walker, I presume?"

Terrence's face was very red and his voice was harsh. "Look, Mac, you'd better come back later, okay? Or tomorrow or next week."

Maybe Terrence was older and tougher than Jonas had thought, or maybe he just hated the Snow Queen, but never mind either one of them. Jonas's concern was elsewhere. "Just tell me," he said. "Did this other man who was in here give you his name?"

"I don't think so—no, I'm sure not. He just took off, like I'd do if I had any sense! This fucking business!" Terrence stormed. "Do you know how many asses you have to kiss every day? And I could have been in Hollywood now, if this cretin chick I was living with hadn't wrecked my wheels—"

The intercom on Terrence's desk clicked and he swallowed his tongue. A man's voice fired out of the intercom. "Terrence, get in here."

"Yes, sir." Terrence jumped to obey.

Jonas spoke quickly. "Maybe you're right. I'll come back a little later."

But Terrence didn't even hear him.

The moment the door shut, Jonas moved to Terrence's desk, where he flipped the cards of a phone index until he found the number he wanted. Then he picked up his raincoat and hurried out to the elevators.

A couple of minutes later Jonas was on the sidewalk, waiting for a stoplight and dodging the splash from cars. Across the street he turned left, walking as fast as he could without losing his footing as he moved downhill toward Pioneer Square. He could see a favorite restaurant ahead and he was hungry, but there was no time for lunch now. He spotted the bookstore he'd remembered from his last time in town and hurried inside.

The salesman eyed Jonas's wet hands and dripping coat with disfavor, but Jonas strode right past him. "You've got maps here, don't you? Charts? I know the quadrangle I want, for one—don't worry, I'll buy it."

The man quickly found him the government map he wanted and then dug out a tourist road map of the same area, along with a ferry schedule for the Washington State ferries. If Jonas had had a chance to do his homework this week for navigation school, he might not have needed the maps at all. Starfish was what he was looking for, the island that was apparently owned by someone named Trevor Vance. It was the name Starfish that had caught Jonas's attention, back in that office.

He spread out the maps on a table. Starfish was a tiny island, not much more than a mile long and maybe half that in width. It was, as Jonas had remembered, only five or six miles from Jonas's own island, but there were others in between. What he wasn't sure of was the proximity of Starfish to a much bigger neighbor island called Shipwreck. But now Jonas saw the probable reason for Starfish's name, because the small island practically clung to the underside of Shipwreck, its big and populous neighbor. The channel between them wasn't really a channel at all. It was marked as less than four fathoms at mean low tide, and at one point it was no more than a hundred yards wide.

Jonas turned quickly to the more recent road map. He saw that there was a bridge or causeway connecting little Starfish to Shipwreck. Both the bridge and the only road shown on Starfish were marked PRIVATE. But apparently it was an easy matter to get from one island to the other, at least for Trevor Vance or whoever else lived on his private domain. And so that would be their regular means of reaching the outside world, via Shipwreck Island.

Jonas didn't really need to look at the ferry schedule. That part he already knew. But he double-checked it anyway, just to make sure. And, yes, the last ferry of every evening, including weekends, departed from the mainland and then stopped at Shipwreck before proceeding to its final destination on Jonas's own island, Whale Harbor.

That was the ferry on which Wilbur Styles had traveled Sunday night.

And so had Wilbur's murderer.

7 "Hello?"

The voice on the telephone was that of a young girl, warm and friendly and eager. She answered on only the second ring.

"Hello," Jonas said. "Is this the Vance residence?"

"Yes," she said. Maybe she had expected a different caller. Now she seemed to be holding her breath.

"Is Mr. Vance there, please? Mr. Trevor Vance?"

"Oh." She sounded disappointed. "No, I'm sorry, he's—he's out just now."

"When do you expect him back?"

The lovely voice was slightly less warm and several years older. "I'm really not sure. Who is this calling, please?"

Jonas pulled the door of his phone booth more tightly shut. The booth was in the lobby of a big apartment hotel, where he had come because he knew they'd have the phone book which he wanted to consult, the book with the island numbers in it. He'd found there v.as no listing for Trevor Vance, either on Shipwreck or Starfish; in fact, there was no mention of Starfish at all. So the number he had taken from Terrence's phone index was an unlisted one. That, thought Jonas, was real privacy, to live on your own island with an unlisted telephone number. But it made a difference in how he handled this, in how truthful he would have to be. Very, he decided.

"My name is Duncan," he said, "Jonas Duncan."

"Oh," she said, and it almost had a question mark after it. "I'm sorry, I guess I haven't heard Mr. Vance mention your name," she added bluntly.

"I thought he might have, in the last day or two," Jonas said, even more bluntly.

"Well, Mr. Vance hasn't been . . . I mean, no, I don't think so. Why would he?"

Because deputy sheriffs can read ferry schedules too, Jonas thought. Because Grayson's men must have been asking questions all over Shipwreck; they must have already talked to every ticket seller and crewman and local passenger who might have spotted Wilbur Styles and/or his pursuer that night, boarding that fateful ferry. But it would be nice to learn that Jonas's own name hadn't been mentioned, like it was all over Walla Walla. "It's not important," he said. "I just thought someone might have said something."

"Are you a friend of Mr. Vance's?" she asked. "Or did you want to talk to him about business of some sort."

Jonas almost laughed. He had intended to do the fishing here, but she was doing it better and faster. She sounded less and less like a youngster. Jonas suddenly became garrulous. "Oh, neither one," he said. "But in a way I'm sort of a neighbor." And he told her where he lived, in his friendliest voice, and mentioned his painting, and said he simply wanted to meet Mr. Vance and talk with him about boats, among other things, for Jonas had heard of Vance's wonderful feat of sailing all alone around the world.

"Oh, God," she said, "that was years ago. Really, Mr. Duncan, he doesn't sail any more at all. So now if you'll excuse me, I'm trying to keep this phone free—"

Jonas interrupted before she could hang up. "Look, I'm sorry, I didn't mean to go on like that. And I wouldn't have called your private number, Mrs. Vance, except a mutual friend—"

"Oh, I'm not Mrs. Vance." Her voice was momentarily a girl's again; it almost giggled.

"Well, if she's there, perhaps I could leave my message with her. You see, it's just occurred to me that I may have met Mrs. Vance once."

"I'm sorry," said the voice on the telephone, "but she went to Seattle to look—well, I just don't know when she'll be back, or Mr. Vance either."

"She has lovely green eyes, I remember. Isn't that right?"

There was a dead silence. Finally, stiffly, "I'm sure they're very lovely. But if you don't mind, Mr. Duncan, I'm just the housekeeper here."

And she hung up on him.

So that was it. No wonder the Snow Queen had been so mad at Terrence Fall! Jonas should have realized who Mrs. Vance was, as soon as she walked in on them. Terrence had obviously been gossiping about Starfish and about Trevor Vance; no wonder she turned to ice. But why was she frightened, as well as angry? And why was the Vances' housekeeper so evasive about Vance himself? What had Mrs. Vance come here to Seattle to look for?

Jonas hung up the telephone and hurried out to the street. He turned uphill, moving back toward Brighton Walker's office building. If he got there quickly enough, maybe she would still be there.

He had gone no more than a block on the slippery sidewalk, however, when he felt the hair on the back of his neck rising. He slowed to a stop, glanced casually up into the softening rain, stepped closer to a building entry, and buttoned the top button of his coat. Fifty feet back down the sidewalk, a man in a gray hat had paused beneath an awning to window-shop. He was a heavy man, Jonas noted, heavier and younger than Jonas.

With his coat rearranged, Jonas stepped out to pick his way across the street and then he turned uphill once more. He glanced across and saw that the man in the gray hat was moving again, also uphill. Jonas swore softly to himself. The man was following him, he was sure of it.

Without stopping, Jonas spotted a taxi and waved it into the curb. But he took plenty of time getting into it. He didn't want to lose the man in the gray hat until he was sure who he was. And so Jonas waited, watching the rear-vision mirror, until he saw the man moving toward another taxi. Then Jonas settled back and told his driver where to go: a camera shop about a block north of the old Snoqualmie Hotel. When they got there, Jonas paid off his cab and strolled into the shop, seemingly in no hurry at all.

In the camera shop he picked up some enlargements which he had ordered of a snapshot Dora gave him before he left Walla Walla. The police had already taken her best pictures, she said, but in this one Wilbur at least looked like what he was, an unhappy loser. In the enlargement he would probably be recognizable to anyone who had seen him. Jonas glanced out the shop window and saw a taxi parked across the street. The man with the gray hat was inside it.

Jonas strolled out to the nearest corner, waited until the traffic light was ready to turn red against the taxi, and then walked briskly across the street in front of it. He hesitated on the far corner until the light started to change again and then suddenly turned to move back along the sidewalk in the opposite direction. Gray-hat's taxi was already moving, forced into motion by the traffic, and a second later it disappeared from view. Jonas turned rapidly into an alley, hurried to the next street, and crossed it to reach the entrance of the venerable Snoqualmie, still one of the best hotels in town. It was where Jonas had stayed last night, after flying back from Walla Walla.

Inside the hotel he picked up a newspaper and saw that the *Post-Intelligencer*, at least, hadn't yet printed any photograph at all of the murdered ex-convict. In fact, the only story in the newspaper today about the death of Wilbur Styles was on page five, and that was more concerned with a possible legislative hearing on safety on the older ferries.

Jonas moved on to the desk to ask whether he had any messages. There was only one, a telephoned message which had just been stuck in Jonas's box. "Your roof still leaks," it said. "Better make peace with the weatherman." It was signed *Charlie*.

"Who's Charlie?" asked a voice at Jonas's elbow. He turned to see a slight, white-haired, scholarly-looking man. Jonas grinned. The man's name was

52

Fred and he was the security supervisor at the hotel. Jonas had known Fred for many years, ever since they first met at a police convention in San Diego. Fred was on the Seattle force, back in those days.

"Who told you to read my mail?" Jonas asked.

"I thought there might be money in it," said Fred.

"Come on, who?"

Fred sighed. "Nobody. But there are some perfectly nice people in blue who cooperate with your sheriff friends over on the islands. They want a fatherly eye kept on you, that's all."

Jonas checked him and nodded toward the newsstand across the lobby, where the man in the gray hat was now coming into view and starting to examine the girlie magazines with morbid intensity. Jonas was sure that he had shaken the man outside. So obviously the man already knew where Jonas was staying and had headed straight for the hotel after losing his tail. That's all Jonas had wanted to find out. He felt outraged, but it was a relief to know who the man must be.

"He doesn't look much like my father, though," Jonas said. "Do you know him?"

Fred looked. "No."

"Well, how about striking up an acquaintance? I'm going to my room now, to change my shirt and make some phone calls. I'll have room service send up some beer in about an hour, so come on up then and tell me what he said."

"Buddy, don't try so hard to get me in trouble."

"Why do you think I stay here, when I'm in town?"

"Because I get you a rate."

"Fred, all you have to do is tell him the truth: first,

53

that he's the worst tail I ever saw; second—here's a message he can pass along—that I'll get in touch with Captain Grayson himself this afternoon. I'll have a lead for Grayson and it will be a good lead. In the meantime, let's stop wasting the taxpayers' money violating my civil rights. Okay?"

Jonas started to move toward the elevators. Fred moved a few steps with him. "Nobody's read your messages but me," said Fred, "and I only asked who Charlie was."

"He's the guy who carved that belt buckle I gave you last Christmas. Won't it hold your pants up?"

"It's beautiful," Fred said, "but so is Charlie's advice. You've got no business in their case, Jonas. I mean, just because you feel guilty about not remembering that guy—and Grayson probably knows it—"

"I just told you, didn't I? All I want is to get Grayson this lead. So if you'll keep the flies off me—"

"All right, all right." Fred sighed, stopping.

"Thanks. My room is five-oh-four," Jonas called back. "See you soon."

Fred waved and Jonas stepped into the most crowded of four elevators. He punched the button for the fifth floor so it would show on the board down below when the elevator stopped there. Then he rode up to the third floor, got out, and walked down to the second floor, where there was another exit from the hotel to a different street level. A moment later he was stepping into a taxi and giving the driver the address of Brighton Walker's office building. Jonas didn't even need to glance back to be sure that there was no one following him now. Fred would be seeing to that, bending the ears beneath the gray hat, passing on Jonas's message in the lengthiest manner possible. Jonas made a mental note. Next Christmas, Fred deserved something even nicer from Charlie's studio. A desk-size totem pole maybe, for the man whose only family was a hotel.

8 Terrence Fall
was alone in the plush reception room, watering in-
door plants. He was no longer inclined to be helpful.
When Jonas showed him the enlarged photograph of
Wilbur Styles, the young man only stared at it and
shook his head. "I don't know," he said coldly. "I
don't remember ever seeing that man before."

"Yes, you do," said Jonas. "He's the man who was
in here several days ago looking for a job. He asked
you questions about that boat in the picture, and also
about Trevor Vance."

Terrence took the photograph and sat down behind his desk to look at it under better light. "It's not
a very good photograph," he said. "Really, I just can't
tell whether it's the same man or not."

Jonas noticed that Terrence was moving his knee
against the inside of his desk. There was probably a
button there. For a buzzer somewhere.

"Who told you to have such a bad memory?" Jonas
asked. "Your boss?"

"Oh, no. Of course not."

"Or was it the lady who was so mad at you? Look,
I'm sorry if I got you in trouble with my questions
about Vance."

husband, Mrs. Vance? I'd like to see him as quickly as possible."

"You—oh, you would!" She sounded even more outraged, but the nervous glance she exchanged with Brighton Walker corroborated the guess that Jonas had been making. "By what right—?"

"Or do you even *know* where he is?" Jonas said.

"What?" she gasped.

"From the things your housekeeper said, or didn't say, on the telephone half an hour ago, I gathered that—"

"Telephone! You called?"

"—I gathered she was either lying about your husband's not being there or else he's gone someplace without telling her."

"Why, that little bitch!"

"I even had the impression that your husband might be missing, might have disappeared. But naturally if you know where I can find him—?"

"It is none of your damn business!"

"Cynthia, wait!" Walker interrupted sharply. "Are you a police officer, Duncan?"

"No."

"Private investigator of some sort?"

"No."

"But you were showing Terrence Fall a photograph, out there. Why?"

"Yes. This one." Jonas stepped quickly to hold his photograph for Mrs. Vance to see first, rather than Walker. But she only stared blankly at it while Walker moved to look at it over her shoulder. He showed even less response, though with Walker that probably didn't mean much.

"It's the man who was crushed by the ferry Sunday night," Jonas said.

"Oh!" she said and reached for reading glasses from her purse to take a closer look at the photograph. But the glasses didn't seem to make any difference; she still didn't seem to recognize him.

"His name was Wilbur Styles," Jonas said.

"Yes, I read about it in the newspaper. So that's what he looked like," she said. "Some sort of convict, wasn't he?"

There was still no recognition but her voice was softer, and as she glanced at the photograph once more she shuddered. Almost with sympathy, Jonas thought.

"What a hideous way to die."

"Yes," Jonas said.

"But he was shot first, the paper said. Maybe he didn't feel much."

Brighton Walker reached to take the photograph out of her hand. "Never mind that, Cynthia," he said. "Duncan, I asked you a question. What are you up to with all this?"

"I want to know who killed that man. And since he may have spoken to Mrs. Vance's husband, or even been out there on the island trying to see him—"

"Oh, no," she gasped, "I'm sure not. I'm sure that man was never anywhere near Starfish, never anywhere near our island, never anywhere near Trevor!"

"And if he had been, Duncan, I'm damned if I can see why *you* should be concerned!"

Jonas ignored Brighton Walker and sat down beside Mrs. Vance. He spoke rapidly but as simply and warmly as he could. He told her the truth about who he was and why he was interested in Styles's death. He told her about Wilbur's telephone call to Dora, in which Wilbur said he had located someone who might help him, located that person just by accident through another name on his list—and that other name must have been Brighton Walker's.

Mrs. Vance was startled. "Why on earth would a man like that have your name, Brig?"

Walker gestured vaguely. "Christ, I don't know."

But Wilbur Styles had come here, come up to this office several days ago, Jonas pointed out. Jonas was sure of that, whether Terrence Fall would admit it now or not. Because Terrence told Jonas earlier that a man of Wilbur's general description had asked questions about the framed picture of the sailboat, the ketch which Wilbur must have recognized from the past—and then he asked questions about its owner, Trevor Vance, who therefore must have been the person Wilbur told his wife about on the telephone.

"Get that creature back in here," Mrs. Vance suddenly snapped to Walker. "He didn't tell *us* all that."

"Terrence is scared to death he'll be fired for gossiping, that's all," Walker soothed. "I'll get the truth out of him, don't worry."

"It doesn't make much difference," Jonas said. "I'm pretty sure that's what happened. Aren't you?"

He looked very directly at Cynthia Vance, and for a moment she stared back at him. But then her green eyes wavered. She gulped the rest of her drink. "Oh, Jesus," she said in sudden misery.

"So now you understand why I want to talk to your husband," Jonas concluded quietly.

"I guess so," she mumbled, turning her face away.

Brighton Walker watched her worriedly, then turned briskly to Jonas. "Well, I don't," Walker barked, "unless you're planning to write a book, maybe. Sell Trevor's story to the highest bidder. Sell *him* to the highest bidder. Yes. Get yourself another job with the police, maybe. Duncan, I think we've heard about enough—"

"Oh, shut up, Brig," said Mrs. Vance. And he did.

Jonas waited. Then finally she looked at him again and waved the empty glass in her hand. "My husband," she said, trying to smile and not succeeding, "my husband has this little drinking problem, you see. . . ."

Her voice caught and Jonas waited again. This time she just sounded tired and bitter.

"I had a brother once, back in Chicago," she said, "who did everything wrong all his life. Now I've got a husband who has just this one little fault." She waved the glass again. "There are times," she said, "when all the sins there are don't equal one goddamn jigger—"

At that moment the telephone rang. Walker stepped quickly to his desk to answer it.

"Go on," Jonas said to Mrs. Vance, but her anxious eyes were on Walker; she didn't even hear Jonas.

And then Walker said, "Yes . . . yes, right here," to the telephone and held it out toward her, and she practically flew to grab it out of his hand.

"Yes? Hello? Yes, Mike!"

Walker was already diving for an extension phone on a glass conference table. Mrs. Vance held her breath as she listened.

"You have?" she said. "Oh, thank God, where?

. . . Where's that? Mike, I can't hear you with all that music. . . ."

"I know where it is," Walker said, with his hand over the mouthpiece of his telephone.

"All right. Yes," she said to her phone. "Right away. Thank you."

She hung up, almost collapsing with relief. Brighton Walker hung up the extension and gave her a sharp warning glance as he moved past her to take Jonas's arm.

"All right, Duncan," Walker said. "We'll have to continue this later."

Jonas didn't move. "What happened?" He said to Mrs. Vance. "Somebody find your wayward husband?"

"Never mind," Walker said. "She'll explain it all later."

"And who is Mike?" Jonas said.

Walker spoke more harshly. "Duncan, that's all, I tell you! But we'll pay you for any time you've spent, don't worry. So if you'll just figure out how much you want—"

"Oh, leave him alone." Cynthia Vance was suddenly her firm self again. She grabbed up her shoes from the rug and slipped them on as she announced, "Mr. Duncan is going with us."

"He's what?"

"Well, what do you want to do, let him go to the police instead? Before we've even seen Trevor? Or maybe you'd rather tie Mr. Duncan up and lock him in a broom closet."

"Cynthia, don't talk that way!"

"Or throw him out the window, maybe? And when

we get there, who's going to help Mike, in case he needs help, raising the royal dead? You? Mike hasn't even got Trevor out of that place yet, whatever it is!"

And then she turned to Duncan and looked into his eyes for a long moment, trying to look deeper.

"Please," she said, "if I tell you the truth, will you help me? Will you promise not to say anything to the police until Trevor is home and safe? Until we know what has happened to him?"

"I'll do what I can," Jonas said. "I can't make any promises, but it's your husband I want to talk to first."

She took a breath. "So do I," she said. "Because, you see, Trevor has been missing ever since day before yesterday."

"Since before Wilbur Styles was murdered?"

"I don't know," she said. "Maybe. But Mr. Duncan, I have no idea whether they knew each other, or ever talked to each other, or met each other, or . . . well, I just have no idea at all. You believe that, don't you?"

"I'll do what I can," Jonas said.

9   They went in a taxi because Brighton Walker said it would be faster; his car was buried in the bowels of a subterranean parking garage. Besides, Mike had Mrs. Vance's car and one was all they would need, she said. Mike Kettenring, Jonas learned, was someone who had been working for the Vances on their island for the past six or eight months. Mike did odd jobs like driving Mrs. Vance into Seattle this morning.

But that's about all Jonas learned. He had been put in the front seat with the driver while Mrs. Vance and Walker rode in back. And even with the glass barrier half open it was almost impossible to carry on any conversation, not on such a slippery day when the hiss and splash of a thousand tires fought for attention with horns and broken mufflers and brakes.

Their driver, Jonas decided, was a slalom skier who was learning to hot-dog, and when Walker said, "Step on it, buddy, I'll bail you out," the driver saw his chance to practice. They caromed down toward the waterfront through Old Seattle, as it was newly called by some people. Once it was called Skid Road, a place where innocent logs slid peacefully down to

65

a sawmill, and it was still called that, though its innocence was long gone, when Jonas was a boy and lived here in the Northwest for a while. But the flophouses and Chinese gambling joints he romantically remembered were gone now. Pawnshops and missions had been turned into antique emporiums and French restaurants, with Tiffany lamps and brass cuspidors. Whorehouses had become fashionable addresses for lawyers and architects. It was a civic improvement, all right. But when you clean up a place of old rotten logs, what becomes of the maggots and spiders that once lived underneath?

Several near accidents and skidding turns later, Jonas found out. The taxi was reaching an area where even the massage parlors seemed to be going out of business. There were wineheads on the littered sidewalks and peeling paint on the firetrap buildings. There were tired adult bookstores and an empty X-rated theater and gunshops with heavy bars on their windows. Business of every sort still went on here, but it all looked close to bankruptcy. The wandering sailors and shaky old men and tight-jeaned girls and strolling black boys weren't here just for fun any more, because it wasn't fun any more. Like a nervous addict looking for a fix, they were here of necessity, here to hunt or be hunted. And some were just here to die.

In the middle of a block, not far from something purple called the Green Garter, a silver Mercedes was parked. Beside it was a young man in a yellow parka who was built like a defensive lineman, but that didn't stop passing street boys from trying to bend the car's aerial or knock down its radiator ornament. The big guy was just chasing a couple of them off when he spotted the taxi and waved to it and they slid to a stop. The big guy was Mike Kettenring, and the moment he saw Jonas Duncan he started frowning. When Mike frowned his eyebrows met in the middle and he looked even more like an ape, Jonas decided.

"Mike!" cried Walker as he jumped out of the taxi. "Where is he?"

Mike didn't answer. He was watching Jonas pile out of the taxi. And Mrs. Vance was already taking charge.

"Shut up, Brig," she said. "Just pay the driver."

Walker did, with a twenty-dollar bill and no request for change. The driver was obviously curious and would have liked to stick around, but Walker shooed him on his way.

"Well?" said Mrs. Vance to Mike as she joined him on the sidewalk.

Mike started to gesture with a thumb but then swiveled it toward Jonas instead.

"Who's he?" Mike said.

"Never mind," she answered sharply. "He'll help us if we need him, that's all."

"Looks like a cop," Mike grumbled.

Oh, Lord, Jonas thought, does it still show? But he knew it didn't, except maybe to someone who had spent a lot of time dodging cops.

Mrs. Vance was giving Mike's arm a jerk. "It's none of your business," she said. "Where will I find Trevor?"

Mike looked at her with a faintly insolent grin. "Three guesses," he said, and this time his gesture was better aimed toward the purple sign nearby. "They got bottomless booze in there, maybe. Anyway, that's where my bartender buddy spotted him."

She started walking toward the Green Garter. Brighton Walker jumped after her.

"Cynthia, you're not going in there!"

"Oh, for God's sake," she said, "let go of me."

"She'll be okay. Mr. Vance," Mike explained, "he spooks sometimes when he sees the net coming. But I sent a kid in a few minutes ago. Big macho was still there, all right, sailing around the world again probably."

"Aren't you funny!" she snapped. Then, to Walker and Jonas, "You two stay out here. There are times when I'm the only one who can manage him, that's all."

"Wait," Mike said, pausing to send another aerial-bender scampering. But other street kids weren't running. Pretty soon there would be a crowd. "Here," Mike said, tossing the car keys to Brighton Walker. "You guys drive it around in the alley. I've been in this place before. We can haul him out the back way." And he jumped to catch up with Mrs. Vance, who was already striding toward the dingy entrance to the Green Garter.

As they disappeared inside, Jonas turned quickly to Walker. "I'll do it on foot," Jonas said. "I'll meet you there." And he hurried off before Walker could answer.

Jonas walked rapidly past an empty barber shop, a fleabag rooming house where the Vacancy sign was cracked and rotting, a boarded-up real estate office, a newsstand where idlers peered into magazines whose pages were stapled together, another bar claiming topless but it didn't say what, a candy store with windows so dirty you mercifully couldn't see the ancient candy inside, a bus-stop bench where a wino slept peacefully in the rain on his pallet of graffiti. Around the corner it was more of the same. But only two blocks away Jonas could see the spire of a new church and a row of brand-new apartment houses going up. When a skid row gets broken apart it splatters in many directions, and wherever a drop lands, there the fungus and toadstools soon start to grow. But imagine a city where such pockets could be measured in square blocks instead of square miles. Besides, the air was still clean enough to breathe. Jonas was beginning to love Seattle.

He sidestepped a glassy-eyed prostitute and turned into the alley to walk back toward the rear entrance of the Green Garter. He was hurrying because he intended to go inside the place, not just wait outside by the car. But no sooner had Jonas rounded the first stack of trash cans than a door flew open and a man crashed into him. The man was unshaven and ripe, but most of all he was terrified. He had apparently been tossed out of the topless place near the corner and expected a bouncer to come after him, because even before Jonas had recovered his own footing, the man was galloping across the street and disappearing into another alley.

With a scream of brakes, the Mercedes jolted to a stop in the alley entrance behind Jonas. A truck nearly rear-ended the car but Brighton Walker was oblivious of it as he yelled and pointed back. "That's him!" he shouted. "Trevor!" he yelled.

69

Walker's voice was lost in a blare of horns. The running man had disappeared. The Mercedes was pointed the wrong way and blocked from turning. Jonas waved to Walker and dodged between cars and ran into the far alley after the man he was shocked to realize was Trevor Vance. Big macho? Him?

Jonas found himself all alone in an even more decrepit alley. Here a number of buildings were boarded up and a couple of them had been torn down. He ran into a dead end and had to turn back to the barricaded place where he had missed a turning in the alley. He glanced back toward the street. There, in the entrance of the alley, a man stopped abruptly as he caught sight of Jonas. This man didn't wear a gray hat, but he might as well have. He was properly clad, a little bigger than Jonas and much younger. His haircut was neat and trim.

Jonas wasted no time. He couldn't. He hurried on past the barrier, deeper into the cluttered alley. A second later, when he surreptitiously glanced back, he saw that the man was hurrying grimly after him, following him. Jonas swore at himself. In the taxi he hadn't even bothered to look back. In the junky street out there he had paid no attention to other cars stopping. So here he was being tailed again and leading his tail straight toward Trevor Vance. That is, if Vance wasn't so well hidden by now he'd never be found.

Jonas suddenly started running. Behind him he could hear the sound of running steps. Ahead were some piles of lumber from one of the torn-down buildings. As Jonas ran through them his pursuer lost sight of him and slowed down.

Jonas waited until the man was just past him and then reached out to grab the man's arm and spin him around, keeping hold of the arm with a friendly but nerve-deadening grip. The man yelped like a startled kid and then just stood there staring.

Jonas controlled his own panting as best he could and barked in his most professional old-cop voice, "Okay, so you guys won't trust anybody. But I'm only trying to help. There's a lush around here someplace I'd like to talk to first, that's all. And you know damn well this is no more Seattle's case than it is mine. So unless you can show me a warrant . . ."

"Huh?" The man was still just staring at Jonas. He seemed totally oblivious of the grip on his arm. Jonas felt a sudden chill in his spine. The pupils of the man's eyes were too large; he grinned and there were flecks of white at the corners of his mouth. Suddenly there was a switchblade knife in his free hand and his voice sounded as though he were listening to his own echo. He spoke slowly and carefully.

"I guess I'll cut your balls off, too," he said.

Jonas moved faster than he could remember moving for many years. His knee jolted upward into the man's groin with all the force of a released garage-door spring. His grip on the man's arm jerked him one way while a chop to the other wrist sent the knife hand flying aside. Or that's what should have happened, if the knife hadn't caught on Jonas's sleeve and cut his arm. Or what might have happened, if only Jonas were ten years younger.

Oh, Jesus, he thought, as the man's elbow smashed into his face, what a hideous time to make such a mistake. This man was no more a cop than Charlie was. Besides which, he was as wide as Charlie's biggest totem pole. And he hit like one. Jonas landed a good blow or two, but he was never really much of a fighter. What the hell was wrong with him, trying to start now?

A truck ran into his jaw and he heard his coat tearing again as he fell. He kicked as hard as he could and heard a grunt in response but it was a damn small grunt, small satisfaction, and then the man landed on top of him and started fumbling for his knife again. Oh, Jesus, of all the dumb rookie stunts, to die in an alley, to be killed by an insane moose who wouldn't even remember it happened—

"Billy!" Jonas heard from a distance.

Who said it, did he? He was fighting for his breath now; there was a knee in his stomach.

"Billy, he's here! I got him!"

The knee was suddenly lifted and Jonas gasped for air. His lungs. Oh, God, he needed that air. Don't hit me, friend, I'm a sick man, I'm retired; didn't you ever hear of emphysema?

But he wasn't really saying anything and he suddenly realized that the man wasn't there any more. The man was running toward the shouts of "Billy!" and the hideous sound of another man starting to scream.

Jonas rolled over on his face. He made himself do a push-up. One was all he could manage, but it was enough to get his legs untwisted and his knees back under him. He rose uncertainly to his feet. Then he heard the awful scream again and ran after Billy. He was in this now, there was no getting out of it, there was no pleading over age in grade any more. He

72

grabbed a short piece of two-by-four off the last lumber pile, and when he saw Billy ahead of him he threw it as hard as he could.

Trevor Vance was clinging to a construction fence, trying to get over it. Billy's partner was twisting a dangling leg, and Vance screamed again as he fell.

The two-by-four knocked Billy aside but not for long. And by the time' Jonas had jerked the other young man off Vance, who could only cower on the ground, Billy was right back in it. This, thought Jonas, will be the ridiculous end I deserve for meddling in a murder case. But, strangely, the thought almost made him laugh. And when he cracked Billy at least a couple of good blows it felt surprisingly good. Maybe he was in better shape than he thought. Maybe he was even younger than he thought!

But when Mike Kettenring finally came running into view, Jonas was quite willing to let the big ape take over the fight while Jonas pulled Trevor Vance out from under Billy's stomping feet. Mike was obviously in his true element now, and the way he piled into Billy and his smaller partner might have been beautiful to behold, if you enjoyed mayhem. Jonas didn't, and besides he had his own hands full trying to hoist Trevor Vance toward safety. Vance wasn't very heavy but he was flabby in all the wrong places and double-jointed as well; this man who once braved every element, who once sailed all alone around the world, now trembled in abject pants-wetting terror.

Vance had prematurely white-streaked hair that was matted and dirty. His once-brown eyes were yellow and bloodshot. His mottled cheeks were un-

73

shaven and he smelled bad. But he wasn't as obviously drunk as Jonas might have expected. Scared out of it, maybe. Scared almost sober.

Then Mike broke Billy's nose and didn't bother to chase after them as the two attackers fled. A car was coming down the alley. It was the Mercedes.

Mike stepped quickly back to where Jonas supported Trevor Vance. "Get your hands off him," Mike said.

Jonas hesitated but Vance was already pulling himself together anyway, straightening up and brushing Jonas's hands off.

"Yes, yes, I'm quite all right." Vance's voice was oddly dignified. And so were his cloudy eyes, as he looked at Jonas from a great distance. "Whoever you are, sir," he finally announced, "I am much obliged."

And then his knees buckled and he vomited.

The Mercedes stopped beside them. Brighton Walker was behind the wheel. Cynthia Vance was in the back seat but she didn't look up; she was rapidly writing something. With surprising tenderness, Mike Kettenring scooped up the fallen Vance and slid him into the back seat beside his wife. Jonas started to follow but Mike stopped him as Mrs. Vance tore a check out of a checkbook and handed it out to Jonas. The moment her hand was clear of the door, Mike slammed it shut and then piled rapidly into the front seat beside Walker.

"Wait! Mrs. Vance—" Jonas started to say.

But she didn't even look in his direction. The Mercedes was already backing and filling to turn around, and then it drove away, leaving Jonas Duncan standing in the alley. He looked at the check in his hand.

It was drawn to him and she had spelled his name right. It was a check for one thousand dollars.

In his last glimpse of Cynthia Vance, she was putting her arms around her husband, pulling him close, holding his head against her breast. She wasn't the Snow Queen any more. Maybe she never was. As the car drove away she was crying, sobbing into her husband's matted and filthy hair.

10

"They drove off and left me too," Brighton Walker said. "Just dumped me in front of my building and took off." He stopped talking as a white-aproned waiter appeared beside them bearing little plates of cheese squares and toothpicked sausages which he deposited beside their drinks with a flourish of extra cocktail napkins. "All right," Walker mumbled impatiently, but the waiter wasn't about to be hurried.

Walker must pay his dues here, Jonas thought. They were in the Klondike Club, which was located on Alaskan Way, naturally, and they had the very best table by the window overlooking the harbor. The rain had stopped and the sky was clearing just enough so there might be a sensational sunset in another hour, complete with pink snow on the distant Olympics, if only the tinted window glass didn't turn it all into Polaroid black and white.

"That's what you get for being an officer of the club." Walker sighed half jokingly, and not at all modestly, but the waiter only smiled and emptied an already empty ashtray and otherwise went on with his elegant routine.

"Pretty impressive," Jonas said. "But if that's the case, why didn't you vote against the dark glass?"

"What?" Walker had no idea what Jonas meant, but he reached out to tap the window anyway. "Beautiful, isn't it? Latest shade. Hate to tell you what it costs per square foot."

"I'm an awning man myself," Jonas said. He didn't much care whether Brighton Walker understood him or not, even though Walker must have made his boy Terrence do quite a bit of telephoning in order to find out where Jonas could be reached. And when he got him, finally, at the Snoqualmie, where Jonas was drinking beer while the house doctor put a bandage on his arm and a house tailor stitched up his torn coat and Fred alternately laughed at him and berated him for getting mixed up in a fight at his age, Brighton Walker was quick to explain, on the telephone, that he would cancel any appointments necessary in order to meet Jonas just as soon as Jonas was available. Walker was obviously anxious, and it never even occurred to Jonas to turn the invitation down. Just as it never occurred to him to tell Fred the exact truth about what had happened. Aside from his too-close connection with the police, Fred was a scholarly and sensible man. How would Fred ever understand, if Jonas told him he had no intention now of dropping out of this case—and he wasn't staying in it just because of guilt over a memory lapse, either. Fred could never appreciate what it felt like, back in that alley, when Jonas suddenly realized he could still swing a fist, if he had to, if he tried hard enough. Why, he might even win a fight someday! It was almost like coming alive again after years of hibernation, not to mention his growing fascination with the strange inhabitants of an island called Starfish!

Besides, he had always wondered what the Klondike Club looked like. From boyhood legend he remembered that it was very important to be a member because you had to be descended from someone who actually joined the Alaskan gold rush, or at least someone who sold supplies to the miners on the docks of Seattle. And if those supplies were dispensed in saloons and whorehouses, so much the better. Jonas had always imagined the Klondike to be a small and boisterously exclusive club. Now it was obvious that inflation and expansion and shifting fashions in the importance of importance were working their changes here just as in the rest of the world. Or maybe it was only that private clubs were going the way of private cemeteries and Polish jokes. Anyway, there wasn't a moose head or polar-bear rug in sight. The present-day Klondike looked remarkably like a Holiday Inn, and Jonas doubted whether Brighton Walker's ancestors had ever traveled farther west than New Jersey or maybe Worcester, Mass.

"So they drove off and left you," Jonas said as their waiter finished bucking for promotion and departed.

"That's right," Walker said.

"Well, it's not surprising," Jonas said. "They probably just wanted to get Vance out of Seattle as quickly as possible. Get him out of King County, too."

"All Cynthia said was they had to hurry or they'd miss the afternoon ferry going home."

Jonas nodded. "Same thing. Now she's got her husband and the muscle boy back in their own territory, at least."

"What do you mean?"

"Assault, for one. Mike broke that guy Billy's nose, plus other incidentals."

Walker was startled. "But those other two guys started it, didn't they?"

"You'd be surprised what people say when they file a complaint. Oh, I know, they were both high and all that. But the one named Billy obviously thought I was with Vance and so I must be dangerous enough to castrate, he said. Too, he said."

"What?" Walker looked shaken.

"He offered to cut my balls off," Jonas said. "Too."

"Oh, Lord."

"So what I'm saying is, Trevor Vance must have done *something* worth complaining about."

Walker took a long drink. "All right, here's the story," he said. "Those two young men were soldiers from Fort Lewis. One of them thought Trevor had stolen his girl friend. Can you imagine what she must have been like, a girl in a joint like that? But that's what happens when Trevor goes on one of his bottle trips. He thinks he's the big sailor again, the bullyboy, the high-rolling cocksman."

"Who told you they were soldiers from Fort Lewis?"

"Cynthia. She told me all of it. It wasn't just one girl, it was probably several. There are different ways of taking a trip around the world, you know. But I'll spare you that part."

"Why?"

"Because I told her to spare herself and shut up, I'd heard enough."

Jonas took a drink of his own. "How did Cynthia learn all this so fast?"

"She learned it on the way home, I guess. A little

from Mike, maybe; most of it from Trevor himself. She telephoned me about an hour ago, just before I reached you at your hotel."

"So that's it." Jonas looked out the window. There were at least half a dozen freighters in view and a tug pulling a barge loaded with containers the size of railroad boxcars and fishing boats on their way home and the Bremerton ferry just pulling out of its slip. There was a breeze scattering whitecaps and fresh salt air out there that you could see through. "Nice guy, Trevor Vance," Jonas said.

"Yeah," Walker said.

"When I was little I didn't know a boat from a bucket. Maybe I still don't. But I always figured I'd sail around the world all alone, someday."

"I know."

"Either that or climb Mount Everest."

"I was going to corner all the baseball cards in Philadelphia."

"I guess you got closer than I did."

"You would have liked Trevor Vance a few years ago," Walker said. "That's when I first met him. He was different then. So quiet and retiring he wouldn't even talk about what he'd done. Most people never even knew about it."

"Times change."

Walker shrugged. "One alcoholic is about as bad as another, maybe. But the mean drunks are the worst. Somebody is going to kill him, one of these days."

"You, maybe?" Jonas asked pleasantly. "I noticed the lipstick on your other shirt, before you changed it."

Walker stared at him for a moment. "I'm sorry for

Cynthia," he said. "Wouldn't you be? But that's as far as it goes."

"Just a little friendly compassion, you mean. Nothing serious."

"Duncan, I've been married three times, I support two families. That's a heavy enough involvement, don't you think?"

"You don't look that old."

"Look a little closer. This hair hat of mine is a transplant. Those healthy sun marks at the corners of my eyes are where my cheeks have been hoisted up. I'm a lot older than Trevor, believe it or not. But in my business, when a young man puts a million-dollar deal together he's a genius; when an old man tries it he's called either a hack or a swindler. So me, I stay young."

Jonas was suddenly reminded of the offbeat nickname Cynthia had used on Walker: Brig, for Brighton. It sounded like something he might have made up for himself. Well, he probably had, trying it out on a tape recorder, in front of a mirror, along with his infrared tan. "All right," Jonas said. "So you're old enough to know better. And Mrs. Vance is just a friend. That's the only reason you take orders from her."

"I do what?"

"Isn't that why I'm here, why you wanted to see me in such a hurry? Because now she's got her husband safely home, she wants to know what I've told the police? Or know if I'm going to file any sort of complaint? Or maybe she just wants to know if I'm enjoying my thousand dollars."

Brighton Walker laughed and waved his empty

glass in the direction of the waiter. "Duncan, you're all right," he said. "But you left one out. She would also like to be sure that you understand how much she appreciates what you did. And as for that poor man on the ferry who was killed, if her husband knows anything about it, then naturally they'll get in touch with the proper authorities just as soon as possible."

"Oh, naturally," Jonas said.

"So there's nothing more you need to do."

"Of course not. Just get lost. She'll handle everything from here on. And I'm sure Captain Grayson will show her and her husband every consideration."

Walker frowned. "Duncan, you don't really think they *will* get in touch with him?"

Jonas smiled. "I don't know what I think yet."

"I wish they would," Walker said uneasily. "Because if you're so sure that Trevor once knew that man Wilbur Styles, then you must have said *something* about it to someone else—?"

Jonas interrupted him firmly. "Now *you're* asking questions, Mr. Walker. Let's stick to hers." Jonas set his glass aside and moved the ashtray closer. "Here," he said, "we'll start with this." He reached into his pocket and brought out Cynthia Vance's check. He unfolded it and laid it in the ashtray and lit a match to it. The waiter bringing their two fresh drinks hurried closer as flames leaped up, but Walker stopped him with a gesture. Walker didn't seem surprised. In fact, he seemed relieved as he watched the check burn.

"Nothing to worry about," he told the waiter. "Only a thousand dollars."

82

The waiter put their drinks down with less than the usual flourish, and when the last flame died he grabbed up the ashtray and fled.

Walker smiled. "You know, I told Cynthia that that check would seem rather like bribery, like paying you to keep quiet about something."

"So now I have witnesses to the fact that I turned it down," Jonas said. "Besides, I always wanted to do that."

Walker nodded. "Exactly. I understand. And now what else can I tell Cynthia?"

It was Jonas's turn to smile. "Nothing," he said. "Let her figure it out."

"Good!" Walker said. He leaned forward eagerly. "And so now you're free, aren't you? Free to go to work for me."

Jonas reached for his new drink and turned to look out the window again. "Doing what?" he said slowly. "Didn't I tell you I was retired?"

Walker brushed it aside. "Of course, of course. And you're not licensed as a private investigator in the State of Washington, either. But that doesn't mean you can't accept a gift for helping someone in trouble, does it?"

"No."

"Then let's get something else straight. I didn't ask you here because I take orders from anyone, not even a woman as attractive as Cynthia Vance."

"I know that. I was just pushing you a little."

"Well, you don't need to. Because I'm scared and I need help. I'm in the midst of a very big business deal with those people. And if you're right about Trevor being involved in any conceivable way—"

Jonas interrupted him sharply. "Mr. Walker," he said, "before you stick your neck out any further, suppose you answer a few of *my* questions, okay?"

Walker looked a bit nonplussed, but then he nodded. "I'll try," he said.

Jonas looked back out toward a passing freighter. He spoke easily, quietly, but he spoke very fast. "It was your name that was on Wilbur Styles's list for possible job interviews," he said. "When Cynthia Vance asked you how it got there you said you didn't know. Was that true?"

"No," Walker said calmly, "it wasn't. But I just didn't realize yet how important it might be."

"How *did* your name get there?" Jonas said.

"I had a friend once who was involved in a state tax swindle. This is something I don't advertise, but he's serving time now in Walla Walla. He's given my name to several graduating prisoners whom he thought were worthy. I've tried to help them find jobs when I could. 'There but for the grace of God,' you know."

"Sounds simple enough," Jonas said, though he was a little surprised by Walker's seeming frankness. "But now if the person whom Wilbur Styles told his wife he had talked to on the telephone really *was* Trevor Vance, how do you suppose Styles got Vance's unlisted telephone number?"

This time Walker paused to take a drink. Jonas watched an ancient freighter through the window. It was a foreign freighter whose flag he didn't recognize, but the men on the bridge wore flowing robes and turbans. Jonas wished he could see what colors they were.

"Styles got that phone number from me," Walker

said flatly and Jonas abruptly forgot all about the freighter. He stared at Walker.

"Go on," Jonas said. "When did you talk to Styles?"

"Last Friday. He called me at home after I got back from Vancouver. I'm *not* unlisted, unfortunately."

"What did he say?"

"It was very brief. I was tired, it was late. He simply said who he was and said he'd been up in my office and had seen a picture of a boat he had recognized. He did a favor for its owner once, he said, but he didn't say what sort of favor or when. Then he said he wouldn't bother me because he was sure Trevor Vance would help him find a job, only he was having trouble finding Trevor's phone number. I gave it to him and we hung up."

"Did he call him 'Trevor' or 'Mr. Vance'?"

"I don't remember. . . . No, he said 'Trevor,' I guess." Walker leaned forward. "Look, you must understand that I never paid any attention to that story about the man crushed by the ferry, so I never saw his name in the paper. I just never connected any of this. I never heard the name Wilbur Styles again until you spoke it in my office. You believe that, don't you?"

"I don't know. You didn't react much, there in the office. You could have. You could have said all this right then, the minute you realized it might be evidence in a murder case."

"But Cynthia was there! Besides, it's par in my business never to show your feelings."

"You mean it's par to lie first? To not tell the truth until you're afraid you may have to?"

"Of course not! But some things do get to be a habit."

"You seem to be showing some feeling right now."

"Yes! Because, damn it, I want you to believe me!"

"I'm not the one you have to convince. You can skip the selling."

"Like hell I can! Duncan, don't you realize I'm going to turn that island of the Vances into a condominium paradise? It's the biggest thing I've ever conceived! But I'm way out on a financial limb. Oh, sure, Cynthia has Trevor's power of attorney, but *he's* still the one who inherited that property nine years ago and Trevor has turned into a drunk, a lush. He's already made trouble for us, sounding off to the environmentalists, getting plastered and not showing up for meetings with important neighbors, politicians, zoning committees on Shipwreck—"

"I guess I've heard there's a little controversy going on over there."

Walker brushed it aside. "People always object to progress," he said. "It doesn't mean anything. I can ram this through, all right." He leaned forward, his face taut with worry. "But if, by any chance, Trevor Vance has got himself mixed up in some goddamned murder thing, can you imagine the problems? The publicity? The legal tangles, maybe? Christ, Starfish could be put on the shelf for years! I'd be ruined!"

Jonas seemed unimpressed. "Mr. Walker, what sort of help do you want? And why from me?"

Walker took a drink and leaned back. He looked tired now, and he spoke simply, his eyes watering with sincerity. "I want to know the truth, that's all. I've got to know the truth. Obviously I can't hire just any ordinary private detective to check up on my own friends and partners." He smiled faintly. "Can you see Cynthia's reaction if she ever found *that* out?" He leaned forward again. "But you're in this already, Duncan. You're also highly qualified, according to my attorney. He did some quick checking on you this afternoon."

"Is that so! Well, didn't he ask why? Didn't he also suggest that if *you* knew anything about a murder case, you'd better tell it to the police in a hurry, or you could be in pretty serious trouble yourself?"

"Of course. And I will, just as soon as I get your answer." Walker waved his drink carelessly. "Unless someone has already come up with a solution to the case, naturally. There are probably lots of reasons why an ex-convict could have been killed that have nothing to do with Trevor Vance or anyone else we ever heard of."

"In which case we just forget about all this, I suppose?"

"No!" Walker spoke sharply. "I still need to know the truth for *my* satisfaction, don't you understand?"

Jonas finished his drink and put it down. "Well, there's been no quick solution of Styles's murder, I can tell you that. And there won't be. They've located just about everyone who was on that ferry by now and there are still no witnesses, except to the fact that Styles boarded the ferry from Shipwreck Island that evening. And he was all alone and maybe frightened, a couple of people said."

Walker stared at Jonas. "So you *did* talk to the police this afternoon," he said, "after we left you."

Jonas shrugged. "Briefly, on the phone. I didn't say

87

much about what happened today, but I told Captain Grayson I'd have more to tell him later on. I said some other people might be getting in touch with him pretty quick. He said it better be pretty damned quick."

Walker waited but Jonas didn't say any more, and finally Walker nodded. "All right. I just told you I'll report what I know. I don't like blowing a whistle on my friends. But *I* certainly have nothing to hide."

Jonas looked out the window. The sky was beginning to darken, the water beginning to look colder. "Mr. Walker," he said, "tell me a little more about Trevor Vance. How often does he take off like that? Disappear, go on a royal binge?"

"Well, that's his first runaway in six months or so. I guess he's tied on some pretty good ones closer to home, though. And he's wrecked a couple of bars on Shipwreck. Took a bowling alley apart one night—though maybe that was last year, too. Anyway, Cynthia is always writing somebody a check for damages. It used to really scare the hell out of me, before Mike went to work there."

"What do you mean?"

"Cynthia wouldn't let anybody help her with Trevor, not for two or three years. Trevor was her problem, she'd say, and off she'd go to look for him and haul him home, all alone. No matter how long it took, no matter where it was, night or day, way out in the boondocks or down in some waterfront dive. I finally talked her into carrying a gun for her own protection, but that's the best I could do. Now, thank God, she lets Mike take over sometimes. Apparently he's pretty good with drunks."

"What sort of gun?" Jonas asked quietly.

"The one I gave her? Oh, it was just a little thing to carry in her purse, that's all." Walker shrugged, then added, "It was a twenty-five, I think." He finished his drink. "Why?"

Jonas cleared his throat.

"Okay, Mr. Walker," Jonas finally said. "Like I told Cynthia Vance, I'll do what I can."

11 The next morning was pale gray with flecks of blue scudding through it. There was a splash or two of sweet-smelling rain, just enough to make the deck slippery near the engine hatch where oil had soaked into the wood and he hadn't had time to sand it down. Now and then there were longer streaks of sunlight, and for ten minutes he chased a rainbow along the misty shore of Shipwreck Island. The rainbow won. It disappeared behind jagged rocks which suddenly turned as green as Irish moss.

Washington Sound was a white-flecked washboard, or at least it looked like one and it might actually feel like one to a faster or younger boat than Jonas's. But the tiny trawler was mindful of its heritage. It plowed straight through the water rather than bouncing around on top, its only lateral motion a slow and dignified roll as it angled against the tide. The surface of the washboard was opaque, impenetrable. If you dropped a wrench overboard it would simply disappear forever. If you caught a marauding shark on your salmon line and clubbed it to death and threw it back into the water you would never see the fate of the corpse.

Then Jonas rounded the green rocks which marked the southern end of Shipwreck Island, and suddenly the bottom dropped out from under his boat. The water turned black and transparent and there was no longer a brisk wind against his cheek. Jonas grabbed for the throttle to cut his speed, such as it was, for there were patches of deep olive and umber in that mysterious void below him. And though he had done his best last night to memorize the charts, Jonas didn't trust any map maker to locate every reef and sunken log on a coast like this. Besides, the tide was falling and he could already see beds of mussels and eelgrass emerging ahead.

He steered cautiously into the narrow channel which cut between the islands and through which the tide ebbed toward him in oily, ominous slicks. He could see more and more patches of olive down there —it must be kelp—and then some brighter patches which were probably gravel. He was oblivious of the darker and darker shadows which fell on him and his boat from above.

A sudden wild scream startled him and he looked up to see a bald eagle circling on teetering wings in the gusty free air high over the dark canyon into which he was moving. Close by in that darkness a flash of movement caught his eye: a kingfisher diving for its lunch. Jonas stopped worrying about his dubious seamanship. For there, scarcely a stone's throw off on his right side, was Starfish Island.

A mile-long island isn't much on a map. But a mile-long island like Starfish can have a shoreline you couldn't walk around in a week. There were no beaches visible, at least on this northern channel tip of the island. But there were plenty of rocky coves littered with boulders and driftwood, including some huge logs hurled above the high-tide line which belied today's relatively calm and innocent sea. Cliffs of pitted and tunneled sandstone gave further evidence of nature's violence, and above the moss-grown rocks there were jungles of salal and ferns and blueberries overshadowed by dense cedars and towering Douglas firs. Apparently Starfish had no shortage of water, like some of the islands. Which of course would make it that much more attractive to real estate developers with visions of condominiums and retirement villages.

Oh, Lord, no, thought Jonas, not here, not on a lovely virgin island like this. Because what he could see of Starfish seemed totally uninhabited. It was not at all like its big neighbor Shipwreck, where even small farms were being crowded out of existence, where motels and shopping centers bloomed, where the big public campground was already filling with summer trailers and the long public beach was already dotted with beach-combing tourists endlessly searching for Japanese glass floats and Russian plastic floats and Canadian beer bottles and all the other strange and wonderful loot of the sea.

Starfish Island was different. It seemed deserted and completely silent, except for the occasional cry of a gull or a jay or the quick splash of a fleeing otter in the water ahead. Jonas grabbed his field glasses for a better look. There weren't all that many otters left around here.

It was then, through the glasses, that he noticed the red lettering on a sign facing the channel: PRIVATE PROPERTY, NO LANDING. He had noticed a similar sign on a bluff farther back but he paid little attention. Such signs were quite common, for many of these island properties could be privately owned all the way down to the low-tide line, and with the thousands of pleasure boats that migrated to these waters it was necessary to warn people off. But now through the glasses he could read the smaller print, and it wasn't just "Trespassers Will Be Prosecuted" but also "No Landing Under Any Circumstances: Violators May Be Shot." There were similar signs every few hundred yards or so, Jonas would later discover, standing guard around Starfish Island like angry Doberman pinschers.

Jonas lifted his field glasses to look at the high, narrow bridge which was now coming into view. Its rickety one lane was also adorned with red signs, and at the far end of the bridge, where it connected with Shipwreck Island, there was a closed wooden gate.

The sun came out at that moment and a tiny flick of light made Jonas swing his glasses close to the right, toward a patch of high ferns on the nearby wooded slope. There he saw another flick of reflected light, and another beside it, so that the light looked double.

He suddenly realized that he was looking straight into another pair of field glasses in the hands of someone who must have been watching Jonas for some time. But the moment Jonas looked in that direction, the pinpoints of light disappeared and the ferns stirred slightly and were motionless again. Whoever it was had dropped completely out of sight. An army could drop out of sight in that kind of undergrowth.

Hell. It was one thing to snoop, another to be

caught snooping. Jonas kept his field glasses to his eyes and slowly lifted them toward the sky as though he were watching the flight of a bird. He lowered his glasses and looked for other birds, feeling more and more exposed every minute. He was sure that the ferns never moved again. Perhaps whoever it was up there was just as anxious as he was not to be seen spying. On the other hand, whoever it was could hit him with a spitball, let alone a rock or a bullet—and so Jonas continued his apparently innocent nature study for only a short nervous moment before he made a show of looking at his watch and regretfully turning his boat around to head back toward the open sound. He could feel eyes drilling into his back as he slowly moved away.

His strange welcome to Starfish wasn't quite over, however. As he neared the rocks bordering the southern entrance of the channel, he casually looked back through his field glasses for one final view of the hillside. As a result, he paid slight attention to the approaching sound of another boat. When he did glance in its direction, he saw that it was a fast small boat which threw a lot of white water but was obviously on a course farther out, heading south from somewhere on Shipwreck to parts unknown. But then the sound of its engine changed slightly, and the next time he glanced back it was to discover that the boat was heading straight toward his stern and gaining rapidly.

His first thought was that someone who knew him was trying to overtake him, and so he waved to the oncoming boat. But no one waved back, the boat didn't slacken speed, and as it moved into his plodding wake it started zigzagging like a water skier, its flared bow sending jets of white water out first to one side and then to the other. Jonas had no air horn. His startled "Get away, you goddamned fool!" might as well have been yelled under water—and it almost was, as the fast boat took a final skidding swing across his stern to pass him and throw spray all over him.

A split second later the boat's wake hit the trawler and practically rolled it over. As Jonas grabbed for a railing and missed and fell down on his wet butt he could see behind the boat's windscreen for the first time. Its sole occupant was standing up to look back —and she burst into laughter, for it was a girl, a long-legged girl with long blond hair, a girl in a denim windbreaker and blue jeans that must have been painted on. With one hand behind her she spun the wheel of her boat to circle him, still laughing and now waving and pointing, still carelessly standing as her boat bounced wildly back across its own wake at full speed. She was a bareback rider, a kid on a skateboard, a mermaid surfer, and as Jonas picked himself up from the slippery place on his deck he felt about a hundred and five.

She circled him, pointing with her free hand again, this time in a slightly different direction, pointing between the boats somewhere. She looked high and excited and the hell with her. Jonas gestured her away as he grabbed his wheel to straighten his own course. She dashed off a short distance but then pointed back and swung into another turn. Okay, you little hot-rod bitch, he thought, it's not that funny—

And then he abruptly stopped thinking and his heart stopped beating as the place where she was pointing, the whole surface of the sound right next to his boat, seemed to rise right up into the air. Seeing white beneath the falling water, his first thought was shark, but my God no shark was ever that big and the white was rolling into black and a huge black fin rose higher than he was as it rolled over toward him and there was a tunnellike blow hole spraying and maybe clicking. It was the biggest killer whale he had ever seen, as long as the trawler itself, and when its flukes rose and the whale disappeared with a slap, the spray fell like hailstones on Jonas's deck.

Jonas started breathing again. His cramped fingers on the wheel were white, and he noticed that his other hand had grabbed the engine control, knocked the diesel out of gear without his even knowing it. The trawler was slowing, rolling—and then he heard a shout from the other boat and the girl was pointing again to the other side and he whirled to see another whale rising and falling in the water. Beyond it was still another. There was a roar from the girl's engine, and her boat nearly sliced off Jonas's bow as she headed straight toward the high fin of a third whale. She was out of her mind; she was totally insane. It was a whole pack of whales and she was heading straight into their midst—and then Jonas caught his breath again as one of the killers shot straight up into the air and fell with a splash and bang to send terror to the bottom of the sea.

The girl cut her speed the moment the whale started its leap. She swung quickly into a circle, slowing all the time, coming up again behind Jonas's stern. When she was thirty or forty feet away she set her own engine to idle and jumped up onto the forward deck of her bouncing boat. She grabbed the end of a coiled line, and when her bow splashed within five or six feet she leaped like a dancer to the short afterdeck of the rolling trawler.

Jonas lurched to grab for her hand but she was already dropping down beside him, throwing her end of the line around a stern cleat in a couple of quick, expert hitches. Jonas was glad he had finally got around to putting decent bolts on those cleats.

"I'm sorry," the girl said breathlessly, waving with her free hand toward the whales. "I didn't mean to scare you, running you down like that. But I knew you didn't see them coming. You weren't looking at them. You weren't looking at all the sea gulls gathering."

"No wonder that otter was in such a hurry," Jonas said.

"What?"

"Never mind. It's all right," he said stupidly. "But you'll get yourself killed doing that, playing chicken with those things."

She straightened up, laughing, looking off at the whales again with him. There were at least a dozen visible now, their black high fins rising and falling.

"Oh, I don't go that close," she said. "Did you ever hear of their attacking a boat? Of course not! I've done that lots of times."

"You're crazy," he said.

"Of course." She laughed and then suddenly took hold of his arm to make him look off in a different direction, where a shaft of sunlight struck another whale as it leaped high out of the water. "I think they're the most beautiful things there are," she said softly. He could feel each one of her fingers all the way through his waterproof windbreaker and heavy sweater and wool shirt.

"Well, that's sure the blackest black and the whitest white there is," Jonas agreed. The leaping whale disappeared in a cloud of spray. The other whales were starting to move off in the same direction. She had freckles, Jonas noticed, and she was at least young enough to be his daughter.

Then she spoke again, even more softly, as they watched the whales move away. "Wouldn't you just love to ride naked on one of their backs?"

Jonas gave a startled laugh. He couldn't help it, and he couldn't help the sudden flush he felt somewhere. It probably showed, for she laughed too as she removed her fingers from his arm and gave him a little pat.

"You're Jonas Duncan, aren't you. And you're going to see Trevor Vance."

She turned abruptly and jumped back up onto the afterdeck. Her tethered boat had swung around slightly and drifted to one side by now.

"That's right," Jonas said, wondering how she knew but deciding not to ask.

"Pull me closer," she said.

He untied the line from the cleat and gave it a tug. Her boat started to swing around.

"He told me on the telephone you were coming to see him," she said, and she waved back in the direction of Shipwreck Island. "I talked to him from the grocery store. I've been shopping."

Jonas nodded, looking at her boat. "So that's it," he said. "That's a nice station wagon you've got there," he added. It sure was. Its short little mast carried radar. Beneath its raised forward deck there was apparently a tiny cabin, with a head and a stove, probably, and aft in the long open cockpit there was a fishing chair. There were bait tanks and a cleaning board and gaffs and poles bracketed here and there. It was a beautiful little sport fisherman, that's what it was, and its big engine probably drank nothing but the finest high-octane money.

"It gets me there," she said. "I can even shop on the mainland or over on Vancouver Island sometimes."

She balanced on her toes above him, getting ready to jump back when her own boat came close enough, and he noticed that he was right, her jeans *were* painted on, and there was apparently no ground coat underneath, either. She glanced down at that moment, of course, and smiled as she saw his eyes involuntarily flick away from her and then back to her face. Jonas, he thought, you are a dirty old man. He scarcely heard her words before she jumped but he didn't need to, he had already guessed.

"I'm Lila," she said. "I'm the housekeeper."

12

He followed her into a big cove at the south end of the island. Its mouth was a good half mile wide, and it reached inland even farther than that as it narrowed and turned slightly to form a perfectly protected harbor. There were still no beaches. The heavily wooded banks rose sharply from water that was calm and deep.

Lila showed him where to tie up behind her to the primitive but adequate floating pier. A canoe lay upside down on it and a big outboard was tied up ahead of that. On the other side of the pier a large, well-polished cruiser was moored. It looked lonesome and deserted, for the curtains inside its cabins were all pulled shut. On its transom was lettered, VIEW PROPERTY, SEATTLE.

"That supposed to be a gag?" Jonas asked.

"That's its name," Lila said. "Everybody notices, so I guess it's good for business." She made a face as she gestured to the big boat. "It's Brig Walker's, naturally. He leaves it here most of the time."

"Which don't you like," Jonas said, "him or the boat?"

"Oh, I didn't mean that." She laughed. "But he's out here two or three times every week on some excuse or other. It makes extra housework, that's all. And he's the kind of man who always mentions his vasectomy, if you know what I mean."

Jonas smiled. "Want some help?" he asked. She was lifting grocery sacks out of her boat.

"Thanks," she said and handed him one, and they moved along the pier toward shore together. The hollow echo of their footsteps on the planks was about the only sound there was in this seemingly empty wilderness.

They passed a couple of side floats arranged in the shape of a U and Jonas nodded toward them. "Don't tell me Brig Walker moors a floatplane here, too."

"Sometimes," Lila said. "He's been teaching Mrs. Vance how to fly. She's pretty good."

"Tough life," Jonas said.

"I'm going to learn too, someday. When she buys a plane of her own, maybe."

They started up a cleated ramp leading to an old pier shed which was built half on pilings and half on solid rock. Lila skipped gracefully ahead of him but Jonas kept his eyes on his own feet instead; it was too easy to trip on one of these worn old ramps. Then, when he reached the top where she waited for him, he realized that she had been watching him with that same little smile of feminine amusement again. The lecherous mind, he thought, is damned if it does and damned if it doesn't.

But Jonas was also disturbed by something less carnal, and when they moved through the shadowy pier shed he realized what it was. Because parked in the shed were a rotting old dory and a slightly newer boat which had a heavily reinforced transom, there were a couple of outboard motors stored on wall brackets nearby, but that was all. Jonas stopped. That made five boats he had seen here so far, not counting Brighton Walker's cruiser.

"What's the matter?" Lila said.

"No sailboat?" he asked. "Not even a mast for the dory or the canoe? Doesn't anyone here sail any more?"

"Nobody ever did," she said, "not here. It's her. Mrs. Vance. She just couldn't stand it, I guess, at first. And then Trevor lost his interest in sailing anyway."

"What do you mean, 'at first'?"

"Don't you know about Frank Bloodworth? Her brother?"

"Well, she said something about a brother who always did everything wrong."

"From what I've heard, that's an understatement. But he also thought he knew how to sail—until he was drowned, almost ten years ago, off the west coast of Vancouver Island."

"Oh."

"It was a little hairy for her, I guess. For everybody." Lila shrugged. "Anyway, she wouldn't marry Trevor and come to live on Starfish until he bought a power boat. Isn't that silly? Now she flies a plane."

They moved out of the shed to a trail which led uphill through high walls of salal so tangled and thick a rabbit couldn't get through it, let alone a man. The footing was rocky and slippery with moss in the many places where water from unseen springs trickled across the path. It was even more slippery if you accidentally stepped on one of the huge spotted slugs which grew so fat in this lush environment.

"Now can I see your picture?" Lila said.

"Picture?"

"Of that poor man who got wiped out by the ferry the other night."

Jonas paused to fish Styles's photograph out of an inner pocket. "I guess Mrs. Vance told you about this," he said.

"No," Lila said, "but the sergeant did, over in the sheriff's substation on Shipwreck this morning."

Jonas gave her the photograph to look at. "Maybe there are a couple of things I don't know about," he said. "What were you doing at the substation?"

"Looking at pictures," she said. "Mr. Vance asked me to stop by." She studied the photograph for a moment, then handed it back. "Theirs are better," she said. "But that's him, all right. It's the same man."

Jonas sighed. "Lila," he said, "when I spoke to you on the phone yesterday, I didn't tell the whole truth about why I was calling—"

She interrupted him with a giggle and they started moving up the path again. "I know," she said, "you're really a peeping Tom. They told me all about you. But Mr. Vance says you helped him when a dozen headhunters jumped him in an alley, so I don't mind."

"All right," Jonas said, "but what did you mean, 'It's the same man'? Was he here? Did Wilbur Styles come here to Starfish Island?"

Lila nodded. "Three days ago," she said. "On Sunday. It was in the afternoon. I barely saw him,

103

though. He came walking down the road toward the house with old Mr. Bakewell."

"Is that Lloyd Bakewell? A friend of mine told me there's a caretaker here named Bakewell."

"Not any more. But he used to be. He still lives in a little shack on the other end of the island."

"What happened then? Did you speak to Styles?"

"Not really, no. Mr. Bakewell called out to ask where Mr. Vance was, because this man wanted to see him. I just pointed to the house and kept on going. I was on my way out to pick some wildflowers for the dinner table. When I got back about an hour later everybody was gone."

"Everybody? You mean both Bakewell and Styles?"

"And Mr. Vance, too. I didn't see him again until they brought him home yesterday afternoon."

"What about Mrs. Vance. Wasn't she home that day?"

"No. She does charity things on Shipwreck on Sunday afternoons. And then I guess she went out with friends. Anyway, I didn't see her until next morning."

"Was that unusual?"

"Oh, no, she's always going someplace. He's the one who's the hermit."

"And you didn't see Trevor Vance again until yesterday."

She nodded. "I ate dinner all alone, Sunday night. The flowers were pretty, though."

He started to ask another question but she shushed him with a sudden gesture. He checked his own heavy breathing to listen and heard a faint short whistling sound from ahead, then a louder *chunk* and a *whish* of leaves.

"There's no reason *he* needs to know," Lila whispered, annoyed. They were moving into a narrower, even more overgrown part of the steep trail now. "There's no reason he needs to know anything at all," she muttered.

They rounded a sharp turn and there was a much louder whistling sound and there stood Mike Kettenring, only a few feet away, with a huge glittering machete in his hand and slashings of brush at his feet. He was naked to the waist and covered with sweat and dirt and spots of blood from insect bites. For a moment he was motionless, staring at Jonas in surprise.

"What the hell are you doing here?" Mike said.

"Mr. Vance invited him," Lila said quickly. "Get out of the way, Mike."

Mike didn't move. "Sez who?" he said and, to Jonas, "Sorry, grocery boy, we already had enough pigs here today. You've done your meddling. Beat it."

"Oh, for Christ's sake. Come on, Mr. Duncan," Lila said, and she started to lead the way through Mike's pile of salal cuttings. But Mike checked her with his machete and then stooped to lower its point toward a spot near one of her feet.

"Mustn't squash any of your little friends," Mike said, and he carefully lifted up a six-inch yellow-ochre slug on his machete. "How about you, Mr. Duncan?" Mike grinned. "Has Lila put out for you, yet?"

He suddenly flicked the slug up into the air, the

long blade of his machete slashed in the sunlight, and the slug fell to the ground in two separate squirming pieces, spilling slime from each.

"You dirty son of a bitch!" Lila gasped, but Mike was already roaring with laughter. Lila whirled lividly to Jonas. "Do you know what that is?" she said. "That's called penis envy. It really is pretty funny, I suppose. I mean, you'd think a great big lug like him would have just a *little* more than six inch—"

She stopped abruptly as Mike's laugh stopped abruptly. For a split second he looked as if he might swing the machete at her. Then Jonas reached down to scoop up the pieces of severed slug in his free hand. "Here," he said, "you dropped something." And then he smiled. "When I was a kid we only did that with rattlesnakes," he said, and he tossed the slimy mess straight at Mike's hairy chest. Some of it stuck and dripped as Jonas stepped past the big ape and walked on up the path, followed by Lila. Jonas didn't even bother to look back.

"Jesus," Lila muttered shakily, but Jonas only shrugged while he surreptitiously wiped his hand on his jeans. He really hated those things. But he had seen Mike's slight flinch when the slug hit his chest and wasn't at all surprised when there was a quite different sort of laugh from behind them.

"Hey, wait a minute," Mike called. "You got any beer in those sacks?"

Jonas looked back to see Mike hurriedly collecting his shirt and yellow parka from a nearby bush. Jonas spoke quietly to Lila while they waited. "How about Mike? Wasn't he here on Sunday?"

Lila shook her head. "Mike's pretty useless when

Mrs. Vance isn't around. I don't even know where he was that day."

"How about servants? There must be a cook or—"

"You're kidding," she said. "There's just me, that's all. Oh, but Mrs. Vance is a wonderful cook, she does most of that, even sweeping and cleaning, too."

"And Mike is the handyman and bodyguard sometimes, right?"

"Mike is my husband."

It startled Jonas. But Mike came striding up to join them at that moment, dangling his machete in one hand and swabbing his bare chest with his shirt with the other. "That fucking salal," Mike said. "It grows faster than you can cut it." He seemed to have forgotten all about slugs and pigs and meddlers. As they walked on up the trail he concentrated mostly on hand-wiping the sweat off his various muscles. The sight was less than attractive to Lila, Jonas noticed. She was no longer a kid riding the waves of her own excitement. Her glamorous day had turned tawdry; she carried her sack of groceries as though it contained nothing but potatoes.

They reached the top of the hill, and the trail broadened into a meadow which was dotted with the gnarled remains of an apple orchard, and then they walked through a clump of pines—and there, suddenly, was a big old house sitting in the midst of what must have been a lawn once, with remnants of a rose garden beside it and a barn that was half open and converted into a storage shed and garage. There was a view up here that must reach to heaven and back on a clear day. But beautiful as the site was, the house wasn't exactly what Jonas had anticipated. It looked old-fashioned and a little run-down. Its drab brown paint had faded in spots, and much of its window trimming and ornamental woodwork was no longer white. Some of the downstairs drapes were drawn and they looked drearily dark. It simply didn't look like the house where Cynthia Vance lived.

"Where is she?" Lila asked, surprised. "Where'd she go, Mike?" They were walking past the open garage, and there was nothing there but a small cheap foreign car which apparently belonged to Mike, along with a couple of old bicycles and a Japanese trail bike which was Lila's, she said. Trevor Vance had no car of his own; in fact, he didn't even have a driver's license, for obvious reasons, Mike said with a grin. But there was no silver Mercedes in the garage. That was Cynthia's, of course. Jonas was relieved to learn that she wasn't here. He wanted to talk to Trevor Vance alone.

"How should I know where she is?" Mike said. "If I knew she was going to take off I wouldn't have broke my ass like that." He paused to hang his machete on a hook where other tools were stored inside the garage and then hurried to catch up as they moved on toward the house. "I'll take him inside, Lila, if that's what the boss wants. You go fix us some lunch."

Lila turned and dumped her grocery sack into the big guy's arms, and he automatically caught it to keep it from falling. "You go fuck yourself," Lila said sweetly. She reached to take Jonas's sack from him and dumped it into Mike's arms too. "Take these back to the kitchen. Fix your own damn lunch."

"You want your tail beat—?" Mike started to say,

but Lila interrupted him in a seething whisper. They were close to the house now, and both of them seemed very conscious of its nearness.

"God damn you, do what I say!" she whispered.

Mike hesitated, then suddenly shrugged and laid a masculine wink on Jonas and moved off toward the rear of the house with the groceries.

"I don't get it," Jonas said quietly, as he and Lila moved on toward the front porch steps. "Mike's only been here six or eight months, somebody said. You've obviously been here longer."

"Over three years," she said.

"Well, for a pair of newlyweds—"

Lila checked him with a hand on his arm. "Oh, no," she said, "we don't live together; you've got it all wrong. Mike is just something out of my past, my stupid childhood. I married him on the rebound, eight years ago. But when he finally knocked two of my teeth out just for smiling at the mailman, I ran away and left him. I never got a divorce, I couldn't afford it, and after a while I forgot all about him. But then last fall he suddenly showed up here. He fixed a flat tire for Mrs. Vance and pulled Trevor out of a fight in town and the next thing you know I couldn't get rid of him! I told them I didn't want him here, but Mrs. Vance said there were lots of extra rooms, there was no reason we had to even speak to each other, and besides Mr. Vance liked him around and—"

She checked herself abruptly. Jonas followed her startled glance to a front window where a drape was just settling back into place. The old house was very silent, very dark. But someone had been watching him again. Or watching her. Lila let go of Jonas's arm. She shivered.

"Oh, hell," she said, "I just like whales better, that's all," and she ran up the steps.

13 The front door opened and Trevor Vance stood there, looking as soberly dignified as a desk clerk in a Canadian Pacific hotel. He was clad rather like one, too, in proper gray flannel slacks and a blue blazer. But the white turtleneck sweater which he wore instead of a shirt was cashmere and his alligator loafers were probably Italian. At first startling glimpse, any similarity between this elegant young country gentleman and the wreckage in yesterday's alley was almost impossible to see. But Jonas noticed that Vance remained well within the interior shadows as he held the door open for them. And his welcome sounded stilted and strained.

"Well, well," he said with feigned surprise, "I didn't realize *you* were here already. My Good Samaritan, the stranger who held the Berbers at bay until my rescue column arrived. Come in, Mr. Duncan, come in!"

The inside of the house was more attractive than the outside. But it was still pretty gloomy, with most of the drapes pulled. Lila automatically moved toward one of them but then checked herself as she glanced toward Vance and asked, instead, "Wouldn't you like a fire in here? It's awfully cold."

"No, no, honey," Vance said. "I'm sure our guest would rather see some of the other rooms, anyway. This used to be my aunt and uncle's house," he explained to Jonas. "Some of their old things weren't worth selling"—he gestured carelessly to an upright piano and some dreary steel engravings—"so here they are, just waiting to come back into fashion again."

"Would you like a drink?" Lila asked Jonas. "A cup of coffee?"

"No, thanks."

"A diet soda," said Trevor Vance. "Surely you'll join me in a diet soda. Please, Duncan. Help me get rid of the damn things."

"All right." Jonas nodded. But the moment Lila was out of the room he got right to the point. "Mr. Vance, when we talked on the phone this morning I didn't realize you'd already been in touch with the police."

"Oh, of course, of course. It was Cynthia's idea, she thought we should, and of course she was quite right. She spoke to them last night, in fact, while I was . . . resting from my exertions, you might say."

"But they've already been out here this morning to see you?"

Vance nodded. "A man named Captain Grayson. One of those efficient bastards. Nice enough, though."

"What did you tell him?"

Vance laughed and spread his hands and Jonas noticed that the fingers shook. "What could I say?"

Vance said. "I don't know anything about any murder. Oh, but of course Cynthia explained how you'd brought the whole matter to her attention, showing her Wilbur Styles's picture and all. I believe Brig Walker has already told them about the same thing."

"I know all that part," Jonas said. "It's Sunday I'm interested in."

"Well, I'm not much help there either, I'm afraid. Like I told Grayson, on Sunday I had rather a headache—" Vance checked himself as Lila came back into the room carrying a tray laden with soda cans and glasses and napkins.

"I told him about Mr. Bakewell bringing that man Styles out to see you on Sunday," Lila said.

Vance spoke a little sharply as he reached for the two cans of soda. "Darling, we don't need that other stuff. You run along now."

Lila glanced at Jonas and shrugged and moved back toward the kitchen. Vance handed Jonas one of the cans and led him toward another room in the front of the house as he continued. "Anyway, Sunday, eh? Well, on Sunday I had no desire to gossip with an ex-convict, even if he had worked for me once."

"Doing what?"

"Wilbur Styles crewed for me a couple of times. I was trying out a new boat, a big sloop. But that was in San Francisco, over ten years ago. When Styles first contacted me on the telephone the other night, I couldn't even remember who he was at first."

"But he told his wife that you were quite friendly, that you had even suggested you might help him find a job."

"Oh, yes, of course. I quite intended to—or at least

I intended to mention it to Brig Walker someday. Brig has lots of connections."

"But you must have asked Styles to come out here to see you."

"No. Absolutely not. That's the last thing in the world I would ever do. Why do you think I live on an island? Here. Look here."

They had reached a much cosier room, a small sitting room where a fire burned in the fireplace and there were flowering spring plants and some very good modern paintings on the wall. This, thought Jonas, looks more like Cynthia Vance. Her husband gestured toward a framed old map which was protected by glass and which depicted, somewhat wrongly, the northwest coastline and Gulf of Alaska.

"The Queen Charlottes," Vance said. "You ever been there?"

"Not yet. Someday, maybe, when I learn how to handle a boat better."

"That's it," Vance said, "that's the place. That's where we're going, just as soon as this stupid real estate thing is settled. Cynthia and I, we like our privacy. One of Captain Cook's mates drew this wretched chart, by the way."

"Starfish seems pretty secluded to me," Jonas said.

Vance laughed and moved to pour his diet soda into the flowering plants while he explained, "Oh, but never on weekends, Duncan. And in the tourist season? It takes shotguns to keep the picnickers out of our hair. No, no, I've been running from civilization all of my life. And now with Cynthia learning to fly, so she can do a little shopping or visit a beauty parlor in Prince Rupert now and then, if she must—"

"You were talking about last Sunday," Jonas interrupted firmly.

"Oh, yes," said Vance. "Well, like I told Grayson, on Sunday that damn fool Bakewell brought this Wilbur Styles creature down here to the house and just walked in on me! Or sent him up onto the porch, at least, where I was resting my headache and thinking about doing a little fishing later on, after dinner. But here came Styles, saying he didn't figure I'd mind if he just dropped in to talk some more. Hah! That's the one thing I can't stand, to be dropped in on! Well, I don't know what I said but I'm sure it was fast and to the point. Like, Buddy, I'm sorry, I can't talk now, or I'm simply too busy today, I've got guests coming. Something like that. Anyway, the minute I was back inside I locked the door and then went straight out the back door and down through the woods to the pier. And I did go fishing, took the big outboard, maybe you noticed it down there. Only I didn't catch anything and I was still angry at being intruded on like that, so to make a long story longer I stopped at a little oasis over on the mainland, and the next thing you know, somebody gave me a ride to Seattle."

"Where you ran away from civilization again," Jonas said.

Vance stared hard at Jonas for a moment. But his brown eyes were too bloodshot to stare for long, so he squeezed his empty soda can instead. In one shaking hand Vance squeezed the can until it finally crumpled, and then he looked at Jonas again with a smile. "Who are you," he said, "the WCTU?"

"Neat trick." Jonas nodded at the squashed soda

can as Vance carelessly tossed it onto the rug. "I never learned how to do that."

Vance was already moving again, this time into a hall which led toward a separate wing of the house. The little macho demonstration of muscle seemed to make him feel better. "So what else do you want to know, Duncan?" he asked.

"That's all there was? That's all that happened on Sunday?" It sounded so contrived, Jonas thought, so rehearsed, so damned pat. But what if it were true?

"Of course that's all," Vance said. "The one thing I *didn't* want was for an old sailor and con man like Styles to get a look in here. Then I *never* would have got rid of him!"

The room into which he led Jonas was indeed startling. It was an enormous room, or maybe a couple of rooms had been combined. But it was also quite modern, with pegboard walls and a couple of littered drafting tables on one side and a number of easy chairs around a fireplace on the other. Beside the fireplace were large display boards with drawings of waterfront houses and apartment houses and tennis courts and riders on riding paths and golfers on golf carts. On the wall were projections of a marina big enough to entertain the Russian Navy.

"You see what I mean?" Vance said. "This is where Brig Walker and my wife hold their little soirees for bankers and politicians and environmental committees. All in the wholesome name of getting very rich. Could you stand it? Would you really blame me for ducking out to a friendly oasis now and then?"

Jonas didn't answer. He had noticed several photographs of sailing boats, and on a display table there

116

were some beautiful sailboat models. Jonas recognized a duplicate of the photograph he had seen in Brighton Walker's reception room, and there were a few more photographs of the same ketch, plus others of an even larger boat which was rigged as a sloop.

"I guess this would have fascinated Wilbur Styles, all right," Jonas said. "That's the boat you sailed around the world in, isn't it?"

Vance sighed. "My one little claim to fame."

"But how about the sloop? Is that the boat Styles crewed on for you? Ten years ago, in San Francisco?"

"A couple of times, that's right. He was a good sailor. And the boat handled so nicely I couldn't resist. I had no money then. All I owned was the old ketch. But you can always find a sucker for a boat that's made it around Cape Horn. And so I moved up in class." Vance gestured to another photograph of the big sloop under full sail. "Soon there I was with that beautiful albatross around my neck. My very last yacht."

"What do you mean?"

"The next year I had a man crewing on the sloop who wasn't quite so expert. But he'd claimed to be, of course. He was a very good liar. Rather a good coward, too. And besides, he paid me five hundred dollars for the job."

"*Paid* you for the job?"

"Among all the other things he was running away from was his draft board. Remember the draft? Vietnam? Well, I was just hungry enough for five hundred dollars that I agreed to put him discreetly ashore in Canada. I hadn't been up in these waters since I was a boy, but I knew there were plenty of secluded places on the west coast of Vancouver Island."

Jonas turned quickly toward him, startled. Even in the half darkness Jonas could see how ashen Vance's cheeks were. There were drops of sweat on his forehead and his hands shook almost uncontrollably.

"Are you talking about Frank Bloodworth?" Jonas said. "Are you talking about your wife's brother?"

"Of course."

"Why?"

"So you'll understand me, perhaps. Understand us. So you'll leave us alone." Vance's voice was shaking now. "Because, you see, I really killed Frank Bloodworth. It was my fault, not his, that he drowned. I thought I was Magellan, de Fuca, I could sail anywhere in any storm, even with a cowardly crew of one. But I couldn't, of course. I lost him, I lost my boat, I nearly lost my own life, and for a long while I wished that I had."

He stopped. Jonas could almost feel the air trembling around him. "You're probably not the only captain who has felt that way after losing his ship, losing his crew," Jonas said quietly. "But you must be the only one who then married the crew's sister."

Trevor Vance laughed softly. "I know," he said. "You'd think she'd have wanted to kill me. And maybe she should have, right then. But instead she nursed me back to life. She gave me back my life." There were tears in Vance's eyes. His voice was almost inaudible. "Because Cynthia," he said, "Cynthia just happens to be the one authentic angel in the entire world—"

His voice stopped abruptly in a choking gasp as the

118

overhead lights snapped on. They were fluorescent lights located to illuminate Brig Walker's display boards, and they glared down on Trevor Vance as though he were on an operating table. He suddenly looked like a corpse whose white-streaked hair might fall out at any moment, whose yellowed eyes were really made of glass. And almost as suddenly, his ghastly sagging cheeks turned flaming pink and he roared, "What the hell? Turn that off!"

Lila, by a far door, was already gasping "I'm sorry, I'm sorry," as she grabbed for the light switch. But even as she reached it Jonas could see Mike running into view behind her. And as the lights snapped off Jonas heard the sound of a slap and a cry of pain from Lila but he couldn't see clearly; it took a second for his eyes to readjust to the darkness.

"You dumb bitch!" Mike was yelling.

"I'm sorry!" Lila was crying. "I thought they were in the little sitting room. I'm sorry, Mr. Vance!"

"Get outa here," Mike roared. "Go get them some lunch!"

"That's what I was going to do. I was going to set it up in here."

"Then move!"

"Oh, stop it!" Vance cried. "Stop it, both of you!" Vance's voice sounded thin and high, but in the half darkness his shoulders were squaring again and when there was abrupt silence he added with even more authority, "Mike, let go of her. Leave her alone."

"I'm all right, Mr. Vance," Lila whispered.

"Yes, dear, but you run along now. Nobody wants to eat. Mr. Duncan was just about to leave, anyway."

"You heard him," Mike said to Jonas, moving closer.

"No," said Jonas. "In fact, I was just about to ask you one more question, Mr. Vance."

"Well, ask it, for Christ's sake!" Vance snapped with unexpected sharpness.

"Wilbur Styles claimed that he did a favor for you, once," Jonas said. "What was it?"

"A favor?" Vance seemed startled, and then he suddenly began to laugh. "Styles did me a favor? Ten years ago? Now, how the hell would I know the answer to that?"

"Styles must have thought it was pretty important."

"Oh, I'm sure!" Vance's laughter began to sound a little hysterical. "To Styles it must have been a very big thing. Like maybe he got me laid. Or got me a price on a case of tequila, what do you think? Or even gave me a hot tip on a horse or saved me from a social disease by chasing some chippy away from the boat—"

"Mr. Vance, stop it, don't talk like that!" Lila hurried closer.

Mike started to move toward Jonas. "Go on, get out," he said.

But Vance checked his own hysteria as he waved them away. "It's all right, Mike. It's all right, both of you. I'm all right." He moved to take Jonas's arm with sudden gentleness and dignity. "I'm still the master of this house," he said, "even if I'm not much with ships any more."

As they moved back through the house toward the front door, Vance added tiredly, tragically, "I'm sorry, Mr. Duncan. But there's really no need for you to meddle any more. You're looking for something important, like a murderer. All we have here is sadness and trivia."

And lies, Jonas thought. And death.

14

Jonas walked out past the garage and through the little stand of pines and the old apple orchard without once looking back, but the moment he reached the full concealment of the firs which overlooked the slope of salal where the trail led downward, he stopped and turned to one side. He hurried through the dense evergreens, staying well below the crest of the hill on which the house and garage were located as he worked his way back toward the other end of the island. In a few open, drier places where only madronas grew, he picked up speed and even ran when he could. His hands and face were scratched by branches and he tripped a couple of times on rotten logs and once he fell down, but he kept on running as long as his wind lasted and his ankles held out.

He knew that what he was doing was possibly useless and probably dangerous. But there would be no reason for anyone to suspect he hadn't left the island. Not for a while, at least. Probably no one would go out of the house for at least another hour or so. Maybe Trevor Vance didn't want any lunch but he sure as hell wanted a drink, every pore in his body was obviously screaming for a drink, and now that he had survived his visits from first the police and then Jonas Duncan, it was a dead certainty that he would be having it. Or trying to. Lila certainly wouldn't be able to stop him. And Jonas doubted that Mike gave enough of a damn to really care, just so long as he didn't get blamed for anything. Or was that all backwards? How much of what Jonas had just seen and heard was true? Was it possible that one or more of those people back there in the house was just putting on an act? And if so, for whom? And why go to all that trouble, unless Wilbur Styles's murder really *was* connected somehow with his visit to Starfish Island last Sunday?

That was the burden of having been in Homicide for so long, Jonas thought. You couldn't stop asking questions, you couldn't accept people or events at face value, you couldn't accept any fact without biting on it first. And so you kept on asking and asking until some final inevitable answer hit you ten times smack in the face—and even then you did your best not to believe it.

Right now spider webs were hitting Jonas in the face, and in brushing them away his hand knocked a big piece of fungus loose from a tree trunk. It felt like moldy rubber and it smelled musty and ripe, and when he stepped on some skunk cabbage a moment later he almost welcomed its pungent sharpness. The big leaves grew beside a trickle of water where the ferns were dense, and so were the thorns of wild berry bushes when he tried to climb above the dripping jungle place. You could get lost in a small forest like this, just as easily as you could get lost in the gloom of the old brown house back there.

Jonas spotted a piece of culvert overhead, and a

123

moment later he scrambled up into the open on a one-lane dirt road. It was obviously the only road on the island, and by now, Jonas figured, he must be at least half a mile past the house. He glanced at his watch. He had used up more than twenty minutes already. He didn't even stop to catch his breath but set out along the road at a rapid pace. There was mostly dense undergrowth beneath the trees here, but he caught occasional glimpses of the sound far below. And close by in the forest there were occasional trilliums in bloom, and devil's club and wild violets—

He stopped abruptly as he heard a crash of underbrush and then caught a flash of something big and black sliding down an embankment. A bear? No, it couldn't be, not here. Then there was a deep-throated roar and a mongrel Newfoundland emerged from the ferns. There was an answering, sharper bark from another direction, and a split second later a big German shepherd came racing along the road. Jonas swore at himself for not having picked up a stick, but it was too late for that now so he started walking again before the charging dogs could reach him. Not having seen any dogs before, Jonas had forgotten that there probably would be some on the island, and now their barking seemed loud enough to announce his presence all the way to Seattle.

But first things first, like staying unbitten. Jonas walked steadily on. He talked casually but firmly to the huge black beast which almost collided with his hip as it skidded to a stop beside him, and he simply ignored the shepherd, which looked to be the more likely attacker of the two, until it got a little too close and he sharply ordered it to shut up. That didn't work, so he tried an obedience command, while the Newfoundland sprayed saliva and noise on his legs. He roared "Heel!" at the shepherd and for a startled instant thought the magic might have worked, for the shepherd stopped growling and barking and turned its head away from him. But then the Newfoundland did the same thing, and Jonas realized that the two dogs were listening. A second later he heard it himself, the rapidly building sound of a motorcycle approaching from the north, from the direction of the bridge and Shipwreck Island.

The dogs forgot all about Jonas and raced off, barking at the top of their lungs. That motorcycle must be either an old friend or an old enemy, Jonas thought, as he ran along the road to a place where he could scramble down into some undergrowth. He had just barely dropped out of sight by the time the roaring bike, a big one, came skidding around a corner with the two dogs in clamorous pursuit of its wheels and rider. The latter was yelling and laughing as he rocked his bike from side to side and kicked at the dogs. He looked husky and young but he wore a plastic helmet and it wasn't until he and his noisy escort had passed by that Jonas realized, with a shock, that he had seen the rider before. He hurried back up onto the road. The bike and dogs were out of sight around the next turn by then, but Jonas was sure: that big cowboy on wheels was none other than the ambitious and proper young Terrence Fall.

There was no time for Jonas to puzzle over it, however, for at that same moment he heard a footstep close behind him and turned to look straight into the twin barrels of a shotgun. The shotgun was held in the gnarled hands of an unshaven man in his seventies who wore a Cowichan Indian sweater over faded overalls.

"Mr. Bakewell?" Jonas said quickly.

The gun didn't waver. The man behind it only peered more closely through his glasses at Jonas.

"Well, you are Bakewell, aren't you?" said Jonas, even more quickly. "I'm Jonas Duncan. I'm a friend of Bill Carruthers, over in Whale Harbor. I'm a friend of old Mrs. Kelly, she's my next-door neighbor. I'm a friend of Dan Sturdevant, Dr. Sturdevant. I'm a friend of Charlie Tlulagit, the Haida sculptor—"

"Nothing but birdshot." Bakewell shrugged, finally lowering his gun. "What are you sweating about?"

Jonas grinned, relaxing. "I've just been negotiating with those two wolves. Whose are they, yours or the Vances'?"

"Mostly they just run loose and scare people. They're all right. But that dang fool on the Harley, he's teaching 'em bad tricks, letting 'em chase his wheels like that." Bakewell grinned evilly as he gestured with his shotgun. "I might have cured all three of them at once, if you hadn't got your ass in the way."

Jonas shrugged. "What's a little birdshot?" he said dryly. "But you mean that kid comes here often? Terrence Fall? That's who it is, isn't it? The one who works for Mr. Walker?"

"Guess so. He don't waste his valuable time talking to folks like me. But he's always galloping out with some big plans or blueprints, usually on Saturdays—

or maybe he just likes to polish the brass on his boss's boat, I don't know."

"The errand boy," Jonas said. "All right, now tell me about last Sunday."

"Huh?"

"I haven't much time. But there was a man named Wilbur Styles who came out here on Sunday—"

"Jesus Christ"—Bakewell spat—"not him again!"

Obviously Bakewell had been thoroughly questioned already, no doubt by Cynthia Vance or others, as well as by the police. But there were holes in the story which Jonas had heard back there in the house, and Bakewell was the only one who could fill in those holes.

Bakewell didn't really mind. It took very little to loosen him up. Unpleasant and bigoted and even mean as Bakewell might seem to be, there was a lonely widower hidden somewhere inside and Jonas was quick to spot him and play up to him. Soon Jonas's only problem was to keep a few simple questions from inspiring a whole series of lectures on everything from the stupidity of gun registration to the uselessness of local crime enforcement. To keep Bakewell at least partially on the rails, Jonas asked him if he'd mind walking while they talked, because Jonas wanted to see the north end of the island even though he had very little time. And when the dogs came running back to join them, Jonas did his best to make friends with the animals, even while reminding Bakewell of what a hurry he was in.

When pieced together, Bakewell's version of Sunday was actually quite simple and not much help. He had been visiting in town on his bicycle that day, and on his way back he ran into Styles near the bridge, on foot. Styles was trying to figure out how to get past the locked gate so he could drop in on his old friend and employer, Trevor Vance. Styles was open and friendly, and it never occurred to Bakewell not to believe the onetime con man. So he let him through the gate and then walked down the road with him to show him where the old house was. They saw Lila coming out of the house, just like she had said, and after expressing the appropriate comments to each other about the young woman's shape, Bakewell explained that Lila was the housekeeper there and he called out to ask her where Vance was. Lila stopped and pointed to the house—she obviously didn't want to waste time on a couple of shabby old goats—and then she waved and ran off toward the woods. So at that point Bakewell climbed back on his bicycle while Wilbur Styles walked on toward the house. The last Bakewell saw, Styles was going up onto the front porch and apparently talking to somebody there, though Bakewell couldn't swear who it was since by then he was already pedaling back up the road toward his own place.

And that's about all there was to it. When he got home, Bakewell lay down and took a nap, like he always did before starting to fix his supper. He was awakened half or three quarters of an hour later by the sound of the dogs barking. It seemed a little soon for Styles to be returning, but since he had asked Styles to drop by for a drink on his way out, Bakewell walked up to the road to meet him. But Styles wasn't there. Styles was farther on, up at the bridge, and by the time Bakewell spotted him, Styles was successfully scrambling over the gate and hurrying out of sight over on Shipwreck Island. All right, Bakewell thought, so my liquor ain't good enough for him. The hell with him!

What time was that, when Styles fled from Starfish Island? About 5 P.M., Bakewell thought, though it was just a guess. And as for that word "fled," Bakewell sure didn't think Jonas Duncan himself would have moved much slower getting off the island or over that gate with those two dogs jumping for the seat of his pants.

Jonas nodded while Bakewell cackled at the thought. But Jonas knew it was very unlikely the dogs would have acted that way unless Styles *had* been in too much of a hurry, had even been running perhaps. And he certainly wasn't running to Shipwreck to catch a ferry, because there weren't any at that time of day. The next mainland ferry didn't leave Shipwreck until seven thirty and the next island ferry, the one which Styles actually took, didn't leave until eight thirty. All of which meant that Styles had at least three hours of waiting to do on Shipwreck Island. He could have well afforded to stop for a drink. Why didn't he?

"Gate needs some new bob wire on top there," Bakewell said, pointing. "I told Trevor I'd fix it myself, one of these days, before all the summer snoops start risking their fool necks."

They were near the end of the narrow road now, where it made a couple of hairpin turns around the edge of the wooded bluff and then dipped sharply down to reach the bridge, which was still high above the dark channel separating the islands.

"I wouldn't want to drive out here on a foggy night," Jonas said.

"Nobody does," Bakewell said. "That's why Trevor says leave it that way. I don't blame him. Times have changed since his uncle's day."

Jonas glanced at his watch and turned to move back the way they had come. "What do you mean?"

Bakewell took one last spit over the edge of the bluff and then joined him. "People," Bakewell said. "So dang many, all over the place. And the price of property going up like a farting duck. Clem Vance, he died a poor man, would you believe that?"

"Well, not if Clem was the one Trevor inherited all this from, the one who built that big house."

"Oh, sure," Bakewell said. "Clem, he owned three sawmills and a fish cannery once. But they're not the hottest things around any more. Besides, there's always somebody bigger'n you are. He got stretched out too thin, lost his wife, and didn't have any kids to fight for. No family left at all, except for Trevor, and he hadn't been around for years. Anyway, by the time he died, Clem Vance was over fifty thousand dollars behind, just in property taxes alone. Care for a snort?"

They were approaching an overgrown side path which apparently led to Bakewell's own house. Jonas looked at his watch. It was a full hour now since he had left the Vance place and he still wanted to keep this visit with Bakewell secret, if possible. But that depended on Bakewell, too, and the man's invitation sounded belligerent. "You're damn right," Jonas said without more hesitation. "I can always spare time for a quick one."

Bakewell grinned appreciatively and led the way through a short stretch of woods to a surprisingly tidy little cottage. "Ain't much," he said proudly, "but it and the couple acres around it, she's all mine."

"Clem Vance left it to you?"

Bakewell nodded. "Five thousand bucks in cash, too. Only separate bequest in his whole entire will— 'sides Trevor, of course. He got the rest: island, house, debts, the works."

They were inside now. Jonas noticed there was a pair of ancient field glasses hanging on the wall, so old they had brass fittings around the lenses. They would reflect light just fine, Jonas thought. He wondered if Bakewell spied on everyone. And, if so, did he report what he saw to someone else?

"Not that I begrudge Trevor gettin' rich, mind you," Bakewell was saying, while he uncorked a bottle of whiskey. "Trevor come here as a little boy several times in the summers. Shy little kid, liked to play all alone. Borrowed a canoe and sailed it all the way to Port Angeles once. Got the lickin' of his life and first place in his uncle's heart forever. Years later, Clem used to read me postcards the boy sent him from all over the world." Bakewell chuckled as he poured a couple of modest-sized drinks. "I like Trevor," he said, "no matter what people say. The booze, the women, what of it? There's been people tried to set fire to his bridge, throw stink bombs at his house, but it ain't his fault the price of real estate's gone up ten times in the last ten years, is it? No, sir, once upon a time he went around the world all alone, and that's good enough for me."

"I know what you mean," Jonas said.

131

"So what if he sells cut to the real estate sharpies like Walker? That's no worse than bringing in the oil companies, is it? No worse than inviting them big tankers to piss in our pretty little bathtub here. Besides, Mr. Walker's going to give me a real fancy price for my two acres. Why, I might even move to Palm Springs or Las Vegas. Have you ever been to Las Vegas, mister?"

"Wait a minute, Mr. Bakewell," Jonas cut in firmly. "There's something I don't understand. If Clem was in debt when he died, if Starfish was in hock for fifty thousand dollars just in back taxes alone, how did Trevor Vance ever bail it out? How did he save *anything* from his inheritance? Did his wife have money?"

"No, no."

"Well, *he* sure didn't, he says."

"Not for a little while, maybe. But he owned a big boat, remember? And he lost that boat. And just when it looked like he might lose his inheritance too, the insurance company paid off."

"Insurance company?"

"Damn right. That's how he did it. Trevor collected a hundred thousand dollars' insurance for that little shipwreck of his over on Vancouver Island. Some lucky bastard, huh?"

"Some lucky bastard," Jonas said softly, and he downed his whole drink.

He had learned what he wanted to learn and suddenly a lot more. He got out of there as fast as he could and a few moments later was jogging down the road again. It was now over an hour and a half since Jonas had left the big house. But maybe no one had yet gone far enough down toward the cove to notice that his trawler was still there.

He knew the island better now, and he stayed on the road longer than before, almost until the house area would be coming into view. But then he heard the rumble of a motorcycle being started, quite close by, and ducked hastily into the undergrowth. He was working his way deeper into the woods when he noticed an open area ahead and stopped abruptly. He could see Terrence Fall, seated on his idling bike, putting his helmet back on. And then Terrence waved good-bye to someone whom Jonas couldn't see and rode his motorcycle off along a path and out of sight. A second later, its engine roared as Terrence reached the road and blasted off at his usual wild pace.

Jonas's curiosity got the better of him. He moved closer until he could see who Terrence had waved to. It was Lila. She was just turning to move back into some dogwoods and alders which Jonas had earlier noticed were located back of the garage and barn. Lila was in a hurry and she disappeared quickly from view. Jonas turned back into the deeper woods to start circling the brow of the hill. He had gone no farther than a hundred feet when he heard her scream.

It was a single, frightening scream which ended with smothered abruptness and silence that was even more alarming.

Jonas didn't hesitate. He whirled to run. When he reached the open area he skirted it until he came to the first thickets of alder. It took him a moment to find the path into which Lila had earlier disappeared, and by now he could hear a thrashing in the brush ahead, the sounds of a struggle—and then, from much farther away, a sudden, roaring bellow.

"Mike, you bastard! Come back here!" It was Trevor Vance. He sounded drunk already and there was a crash of breaking glass. "Where's the other bottle, you son of a bitch? Mike, baby! Don't waste your time out there. I need you!" Trevor yelled, coming closer. "I want a drink!"

There was a muttered curse from close ahead, a scrambling in the brush, and then heavy steps moving off in the direction of Vance's shouting. Jonas checked himself momentarily as he caught a glimpse, through the trees, of Trevor Vance lurching out from the house and then turning back as Mike came lumbering into view to join him.

Then Jonas heard a soft sobbing sound from close by, and he turned to see Lila lying face down on the ground. Her shirt was torn half off. He stooped to touch her and she jerked as though shot, for she hadn't heard him coming. She had a bruise under one eye and her nose was apparently bleeding. But rage and pain seemed both forgotten in her horror at seeing Jonas. She jumped to her feet.

"Where did you come from?" she whispered.

He started to take hold of her arm. "Come on," he said, "let's get you out of here. You're coming with me."

She gasped and ripped loose from his hand. "Oh, no, I'm not!" And before he could stop her she ran off toward the garage. Jonas followed but he kept far enough back so that the two men who were now lurching up the steps and into the house wouldn't see him, in case they looked this way. But they didn't.

Lila came quickly back out of the garage, wheeling her little trail bike and carrying a faded old sweat shirt. She moved to keep the garage between her and the house, and then she stopped beside Jonas and laughed suddenly.

"Look, I don't need any saving, thanks. All he was trying to do was rape me, and a husband can't do that to a wife, can he? Not to this one, anyway."

She giggled as she tugged at her torn shirt, then ripped it completely off and used it to wipe the blood from her face. She wore no brassiere and seemed oblivious of her own bouncing breasts. But Jonas wasn't.

"It's not my blood." She laughed. "I bit him." She tossed the shirt aside and waved toward the house. "So all right. It's drinky time. Let the boys have their fun."

But as she shook out the sweat shirt and pulled it over her head, Jonas could practically feel the hysteria which trembled in her voice. And when she threw her hair back and looked straight at him for the first time, he saw the tears of fear in her eyes.

"Now you get out of here," she said. "Please, Jonas, get out of here fast. If he sees you still here on his island, when he's like this, he'll kill you! He will, he'll kill you!"

And she ran with the trail bike out toward the road, where she jumped aboard and kicked its little motor into action and took off.

15 It was midaf-
ternoon when he left the trawler in its home berth
near the end of Mrs. Kelly's pier. It was a good safe
mooring place in all kinds of weather, though the
pier itself was pretty decrepit. It had been jerry-built
in the early days of World War II, when lumber was
in big demand and old man Kelly had visions not only
of marketing every tree on his property but even of
cutting in on Whale Harbor's dockage business. Kelly
was going to build a warehouse and all sorts of facili-
ties that never quite panned out.

Kelly was going to build a limekiln once, too. And
before that he found a tiny piece of ambergris on the
beach and spent two whole years trying to invent a
detector which would locate that glamorous per-
fume ingredient from the intestines of sperm whales.
Of course, sperm whales hardly ever came near this
part of the world any more and how that one piece
of ambergris got here no one ever knew. But the
oceans are strange and Kelly was never daunted by
reality. When his wife refused to let him cut down
their beautiful cedar trees, he went broke in the
sand-and-gravel business instead and helped to win

the war that way. Now that old man Kelly was dead, his wife raised daffodils and for the first time enjoyed some revenue from her lifetime of patience and hard work. And she still wouldn't let anyone cut down a cedar tree, except Charlie, of course, for his totem poles, which was how "Charlie's Woods" got its name.

But every time Jonas tied up at the old pier he couldn't help but think of old man Kelly and wish that he could have met him. Any grown man who'd go looking for ambergris would have been a man worth knowing.

Or would he? Trevor Vance had sailed all alone around the world once and look at the mess he'd turned into—or seemed to have. That was the trouble with people. They were never all one thing or another. And just when you thought you knew them best was when they acted most like strangers.

Thank God.

Because what you are thinking, Jonas thought, is bullshit. Maybe it's because you feel frustrated and foolish for being unable to get a pair of pretty tits out of your mind. Or because you feel guilty for leaving the girl behind over there. Or a hell of a lot more likely, it's because you know damn well there is a powder keg somewhere on Starfish Island. And somehow Wilbur Styles set a fuse burning toward that powder keg and he died for it. And the fuse is still burning. Of that Jonas was dead certain. But when and where would the explosion occur? And how could anyone stop it?

Jonas climbed up the steps to the main pier where there was usually a Kelly grandson tinkering with one of the outboard hulls which he and his brothers built and raced. But fortunately there was no one there now, so Jonas didn't have to explain his unfriendly hurry as he headed toward shore.

Since the beach shelved out gradually here, it was quite a long pier. Of course it wasn't really a beach, it was a shingle—in the deeper water a million boulders covered with every form of tidal life imaginable, and closer to shore a billion polished rocks and pebbles which hissed and murmured as they were nudged by the gentle waves of the incoming tide. There was usually no real surf here, except in a big storm, and then all hell could break loose, as the high tangle of driftwood logs attested.

When he was over dry land, Jonas dropped down off the pier so Mrs. Kelly wouldn't see him from her house. He loved the old lady dearly, but she would insist on feeding him high tea, at this or any other time of day, and Jonas had no minutes to spare. While he hurried along the path through the ferns above the driftwood which led to his own little place, half a mile away, Jonas mentally listed the immediate phone calls he had to make: an insurance investigator in Los Angeles who handled marine stuff and might have connections in San Francisco; another old friend down there who used to work in a newspaper morgue; the county recorder's office, though maybe they wouldn't give information over the telephone; Stafford Lewis in Victoria, to find out who kept records of shipwrecks in British Columbia. And last but not least, of course, Dora Styles in Walla Walla, to push her memory a little harder, a lot harder.

He was so busy checking his priorities that for once

he didn't notice the section of his own path which always needed weeding, or the cracked second step on the front porch stairway which he always told himself he would fix tomorrow. And for once he didn't pause on the wide old porch of the small old cottage to look for Mount Baker or to measure the color of the sky. He walked inside and was halfway to his telephone before he noticed there was someone huddled under a blanket on the couch. It was Cynthia Vance.

"I'm sorry," she said quickly. "I took a blanket off your bed, I hope you don't mind."

Jonas smiled. He was startled not only by her presence but also by how relieved he suddenly felt to see her again. "It's not that cold," he said. "Why didn't you light a fire?"

He moved to a Franklin stove and lit a match to the paper and kindling inside while Cynthia unwound her long legs from the blanket and stood up to fold it. In boots and slacks and an Indian jacket she looked just as beautiful as she had in Seattle.

"I didn't have my checkbook," she said.

Jonas laughed. "My corny act. Walker told you, eh?"

"I liked it." She shivered. "Could we have a fire in the fireplace, too? I got chilled waiting outside, I guess. I didn't come in until just a few minutes ago."

"The door is never locked."

"So I noticed. But I still didn't think I should. I thought maybe you were mad at me."

Jonas stooped to stuff some paper under logs in the fireplace. "No," he said. "But that was a pretty stupid stunt driving off and leaving me in that alley in Seattle. Even with the check, I still might have gone to the nearest phone and called the police right then and there. Why'd you risk it?"

She didn't answer, and he glanced up from tossing more logs into the fireplace. She wasn't looking at him, she was looking at a painting over the mantel, and then she shrugged as though the question weren't important. "I don't know," she said. "I guess I was rattled. All I could think of was getting Trevor home."

Jonas struck a match to the fire and rose to his feet. "I'll get you some brandy," he said, starting toward the kitchen.

"Who is she?" Cynthia said softly, still looking at the painting.

"Her name was Kathy," Jonas said, without looking back.

Through the kitchen window he noticed a small car with a sticker on its windshield parked behind his blue pickup and recognized it as one of the two rental cars from the island airport. So that's how she got here.

"You didn't answer my question," she said, following him into the kitchen. "Who is—or was—she?"

"My wife," he said. "She's dead."

"I'm sorry."

"Me, too. Straight or some ice?"

"Just like that, thank you." She took the glass from him and he poured one for himself and they moved back into the living room.

"I like the one of her in the bedroom better," Cynthia said. "But that's her in the far-out pastel over there, too, isn't it?"

"I suppose so."

"And I'll bet she's somewhere in that gorgeous seascape. And even deep in all those soft green ferns on the easel, there—"

"Look, Mrs. Vance," Jonas interrupted brusquely, "I don't believe you were ever rattled in your whole life. But we'll skip the alley scene in Seattle for now."

"You don't like me to talk about her, do you. Can't you even call me Cynthia?"

"I don't like to waste time. Here. Sit down." He tossed a cushion onto the hearth for her and poked at the fire. "You're here for just one reason and you know it. You want to find out how your husband performed today, right? To see how he passed his third degree?"

Cynthia shrugged as she picked up her purse from the couch and settled herself on the cushion in front of the fire. "I'm a little curious about your reactions, maybe. But after all, I was there this morning, when the police questioned both of us. I don't suppose Trevor told you anything new." She sipped her brandy. "Don't I get any credit at all for calling the police so quickly? Didn't that impress you even one tiny bit?"

Jonas sat down on the hearth, moving her purse aside to make room for his own drink, leaving his hand on the purse for a moment. "It surprised the hell out of me," he conceded.

Cynthia laughed. "Well, there. You see? When a person doesn't have anything to hide—"

"Cynthia, where's your gun?"

"What?"

"The little automatic Brig Walker gave you. The twenty-five."

Cynthia reached to remove Jonas's hand from her purse. "Why, you sneaky thing. You really were a cop once, weren't you." She was smiling but it faded quickly. "I don't know where it is. Why?"

"Wilbur Styles was shot with a twenty-five."

She stared at him and her lovely pale skin was suddenly two shades paler.

"Didn't Captain Grayson tell you?" Jonas said. "Didn't he even ask about the gun?"

"No," she whispered. "I wonder why not?" But then she shook herself. "Well, anyway, it was stolen. Out of the dash compartment of my car, five or six months ago, I don't even know exactly when. I never touched the silly thing. The only reason I kept it there was to satisfy Brig. Anyway, there are so many guns all over, these days, everybody has them to shoot their neighbors or wives with . . . don't they?"

Jonas sighed. "All right," he said, "let's skip that. But why *are* you here? If it's not to find out what Trevor told me, or what else I learned over on Starfish, why change your mind?"

"Do what?"

"About me. That thousand-dollar check was to pay me off, wasn't it? To tell me to get lost, to go away, stay out of your life?"

"No!" she gasped. "Of course not! Where on earth did you get that silly idea?"

A spark popped out of the fire. Jonas was glad of the interruption. He poked a burning log back and decided there was no point in telling her what Brig Walker had said to him in the Klondike Club. But he wondered how many more wrong ideas Walker had tried to give him.

"I don't know." Jonas suddenly grinned. "I'm just touchy, I guess."

Cynthia smiled. "Besides," she said, "I already know about your visit with Trevor today. I talked to him later on the telephone."

"After I was there?"

"Yes. He liked you, he said."

Jonas doubted that. "You mean he was already drunk."

Cynthia smiled wryly. "A little. By now he's a complete mess, I suppose. He was so exhausted after all he's been through. But I spoke to Mike Kettenring, too. I told him I'd kill him if he left Trevor alone today."

Jonas noticed that the firelight made her eyes look even more green. And her long hair was brown but now there were strands of gold in it. So he looked at an andiron instead. "Why do you trust Mike Kettenring?"

"Well, I don't, really. But he's stupid and likes money and likes to drive a big car. Besides, Lila can keep him in line."

"You sure about that?"

"Lila can keep any man in line." Cynthia laughed. "Jonas, don't tell me you didn't notice. Surely she wiggled it at you a little bit!"

"All right," Jonas said, startled by his own sudden embarrassment, "but then why do you trust *her?* If your husband chases girls every time he gets drunk—"

"Oh, don't think he hasn't chased Lila! But at least she tells me about it, and it keeps him at home—or did for a year or two, until he got bored, I guess."

Jonas stared at her. "That's a hell of a way to keep your husband home," he said.

Cynthia flushed. "Well, it was never very often and it didn't mean anything. Jonas, we can't all be old-fashioned forever about sex!" She tried to laugh but it didn't quite come out that way.

"You mean you don't give a damn? I don't believe you."

"Well, for God's sake," she said, "I have to have *somebody* there to help me, don't I? We just got her by a lucky accident; she was a stewardess on a plane we flew on once. At least Lila is loyal and works hard and keeps her mouth shut."

"Why haven't you got a male nurse? Trevor looks ten years older than he probably is. What's he have, galloping cirrhosis? Superhypertension?"

"No! I'll admit his doctor doesn't say very nice things. But it's nothing that bad, yet."

"What's his psychiatrist say?"

"He won't go to one."

"How about AA?"

"Don't think I haven't pushed. Oh, but Jonas, you've only seen Trevor at his worst! Don't you understand? He'll go for months at a time without drinking!"

"So what set him off this time? He still looks like he expects the sky to fall. Why? Cynthia, what really happened on Sunday? What could Wilbur Styles have done or said or—"

"Nothing! I don't know! But it's got nothing to do with Styles's murder, I just know it doesn't!"

"You mean you hope it doesn't."

"Oh, shit!" She was practically screaming. She

144

whirled toward the fire and put her hands over her face.

"Okay," Jonas said, after a while. "I'm sorry. But I need more answers. And I guess when I was over there on Starfish I couldn't help wondering how you stand it. Stand everything."

She shrugged tiredly. She didn't look up. "Oh, but I'm going to be so rich someday," she muttered. "Haven't you listened to the gossips? Why else would that snotty green-eyed biddy waste time on a drunk? If you ask me, dear, she feeds him those bottles herself, just to keep him under her thumb until she doesn't need him any more!"

"That makes good sense," Jonas said.

She looked quickly at his smile and then back into the fire so he wouldn't see her moistening eyes. "When we were first married," she said softly, "we didn't even know about the goddamn inheritance. Not until some lawyer finally located us up in the Cariboo country. We'd been living in an old cabin for the whole summer. It was made out of solid gold and Trevor caught silver trout with his bare fingers and fought off the wolves with his bare hands. . . ."

She laughed and waved to Jonas's living room. "Well, when I walked in here and saw all those beautiful paintings, I thought maybe you were the kind of person who might understand about . . . well, about the dumb things people do for love."

She suddenly jumped to her feet.

"Cynthia—"

"No. I've got to go now," she said quickly. "Jonas, the only reason I stopped by was to tell you that I saw Captain Grayson again this afternoon. Here in Whale

Harbor. Because there was one last ferry employee who hadn't seen *me* yet."

"Seen you?"

"Like in a lineup, you know. Only not like that, really. The captain was very nice. And the point is, everybody on that ferry crew knows what Trevor looks like—and the ticket sellers and a lot of the local passengers, too. And Mike Kettenring gets around a lot, and practically everyone in the islands knows Lila, or would like to. And Mr. Bakewell is an institution. But nobody saw us. Nobody saw any of us, or any of our cars or bikes—"

"On that ferry Sunday night, you mean?"

"Well, yes! So if Wilbur Styles was murdered by somebody who was following him, it just couldn't have been Trevor, that's all. Or me or anyone else from Starfish Island. That's what Captain Grayson has finally decided, and I wanted you to know, because I thought it would change everything and we wouldn't have to worry so much or be so afraid of all the things we don't know. . . ."

Her voice trailed to a stop. Jonas was still just looking at her, and she already knew what he was thinking.

"But it doesn't," she finally added. "It doesn't change one damn thing, does it. Not for you."

"No," Jonas said. "Not for anybody."

16 The barometer was probably falling. Gusts of wind cut through the late-evening fog like cold knives. They belonged to February, not early May, and they were slicing all the wispy gray veils into black shrouds. Soon the night air would be almost clear and he would be able to see all the way up to B Street, where there was a comfortable little bar just built for a night like tonight.

Jonas stomped his feet on the cold wet planks and pulled his down jacket tighter around his waist. He wished that he could pull up the jacket's hood, but then he might not hear all the sounds he was waiting to hear. He peered at the luminous dial of his watch and moved a few steps closer to the hazy place where the two high floodlights were. In a thicker fog, those floodlights would be about as useful as candles in a snowstorm.

But then the whole sky around the ancient slip began to glow, faintly, fuzzily, and the sudden deafening blast of a ship's whistle washed over him, borne by the onshore wind: one long blast followed by two shorts. The last ferry of the evening came surging out of the darkness like a portly sequined ghost.

Jonas moved back a few steps on the rickety old fishing pier on which he stood, one of the two deserted piers which bordered the ferry slip. Even without the fog, he noticed, the lights from the approaching ferry were too low to strike him directly here. And if he sat down, as he now did on an empty bait box, he probably couldn't be seen at all, either by anyone on the ferry's busy automobile deck or by workmen in the shed on shore.

He sat down just in time, for the ferry nudged the pilings of his pier at that moment and the weathered planks beneath him creaked and shuddered. The sound of the winch starting to lower the unloading ramp was drowned in a building roar of truck engines. As always, a few people honked their horns just for the hell of it, and unseen headlights snapped on to make the pandemonium of docking even more luminous.

Against that brilliant glow of light, the dark figure of a man slowly rose into view. The man was apparently climbing up onto the pier from the ferry below, and he was a good fifty feet away, but even through the fog he was so sharply silhouetted that he was perfectly recognizable; he was a perfect target.

Jonas was so intent on watching the man that he didn't hear steps approaching from the opposite direction. But then a quiet voice said, "Couldn't miss him from here, could you."

Jonas whirled to see Captain Grayson, who looked both cold and sour.

"Who is it," Grayson said more loudly, "your Indian friend? I never had a chance to shoot an Indian before."

"Hey, Jonas? What's going on?"

"It's all right, Charlie," Jonas called back. "Time out, that's all."

The silhouette danced closer. "Time out! Oh, no, man, I gotta keep moving. My knockers got frozen, lying over there waiting for that damn ferry."

"This is Captain Grayson, Charlie."

"Wouldn't you know. What's the matter, is there a law against us playing Indians and Cowboys?"

"Why don't you go home, Charlie?" Grayson said coldly. "I want to talk to Mr. Duncan, here."

Charlie gave Jonas a quick protective glance. "Well, I'd sure like to oblige you, sir. But the only trouble is, Mr. Duncan here owes me a drink. And so does that ferryboat captain, Ed Murphy. You know Murph was twenty minutes late tonight?"

"I'll be okay," Jonas said.

"Sure you will," said Charlie. "So I'll just wait for you up in the place on B Street." And without even looking at Grayson again he walked off into the fog.

"Touchy bastard," Grayson muttered.

Jonas ignored it. He waved toward the place where Charlie's imitation of Wilbur Styles had been interrupted.

"Well?" Jonas said.. "It could have happened that way Sunday night, couldn't it?"

Grayson nodded tiredly. "Sure," he said. "The angle the bullet entered his body doesn't mean anything. Styles could have been turning, when he climbed up over the edge there."

"So he could have been shot from here, or from the passenger shed or the pier on the other side, or from a lot of places besides the ferry."

149

"That's right," Grayson said. "It just seemed so obvious at first that somebody had followed him onto the ferry. Several people said he acted like he was afraid he was being followed. But he also could have been shot by somebody who was here waiting for him and then spotted him climbing up there."

"Somebody with a twenty-five," Jonas said. "Captain, why didn't you ask Cynthia Vance about her gun?"

Grayson looked sharply at him. "Jesus, you get around a lot. Well, the main reason is she reported it as stolen five months ago. It's right there in the record at the Shipwreck substation. Second, why play a card until you know what it's worth? But also"— Grayson gestured a bit vaguely toward the fog-shrouded blackness of the sound—"there are lots of other twenty-fives. And in this bailiwick, looking for a murder weapon is pretty often a waste of time. It's just too damned easy here for a killer to get rid of a weapon."

"All right, then tell me something else—"

"No," Grayson said firmly. He took hold of Jonas's arm. *"You're* going to answer the questions."

He led Jonas off the pier to A Street, where a sheriff's car was parked. They climbed into the front seat, which was only slightly warmer than outside, but Grayson didn't start the car motor or turn on the lights. Instead, he unlocked the dash compartment and took out a half-pint bottle of whiskey. He broke the seal and removed the cap and offered the bottle to Jonas.

Jonas smiled. "Captain, you surprise me!"

Grayson watched while Jonas took a warming

150

drink of the whiskey. "Are you working for Mr. Brighton Walker?" Grayson asked.

Jonas lowered the bottle and handed it to Grayson. "I might let Walker pay some of my expenses," he said. "It depends on what I find. I didn't promise him anything."

"He's a pretty important man," Grayson said. "He knows every politician in the country. My boss is a politician."

"Most sheriffs are."

Grayson gave Jonas a hard look and took a drink of his own without bothering to wipe off the lip of the bottle. "So now my boss has a new theory," Grayson said, "like maybe Styles was just shot by a sniper. Some freaky tourist from California on the ferry, maybe. Somebody high on hash."

"It's possible," Jonas said.

"Sure. So why waste all this time and money on a regular murder investigation? All we're doing is tying up a lot of our own men and upsetting a lot of nice people. After all, what was Wilbur Styles anyway but a useless ex-con?" Grayson took another, longer drink.

"I don't know," Jonas said quietly. "What do you think he was?"

Grayson lowered the bottle, hesitated a moment. "A blackmailer, maybe. Or he wanted to be one."

"No," Jonas said, "that doesn't quite make sense."

"Why not? He knew something, didn't he? Isn't that what you're finding out?"

"Yes. But I don't know what it was yet."

"So give me a guess."

Jonas grinned and reached for the bottle again.

151

"You sound a little desperate, captain. You have my sympathy."

Grayson looked sharply at him. "Duncan, let's not have any more of that 'you're retired' crap. I can always deputize you, remember. Or I can charge you with interfering with a police investigation."

"I just want another drink, that's all," Jonas said, and he drank it and then put the cap back on the bottle, and Grayson put the bottle back in the dash compartment. "Okay, fire away."

Jonas answered Grayson's questions rapidly and fully. There was no reason to hide anything, at least not any of the few facts which Jonas had learned so far. But he skipped some of his impressions because he hadn't really sorted them out for himself yet. And he dodged conclusions because he hadn't drawn any —except for one, of course, the one that grew stronger and stronger every minute: Wilbur Styles's death was no accident, no chance event, no trivial freak happening to be brushed aside and forgotten.

Grayson nodded. Grayson had his own reason for believing that Styles's death simply couldn't be anything but cold-blooded, premeditated murder. It was money. Grayson had a deep belief in money as the motive for everything. And if Styles knew something that in any conceivable way could have affected the Starfish Island development project, then silencing Styles would have been worth plenty of money. There weren't just millions of dollars involved in that project, eventually there might be tens or even hundreds of millions. Grayson licked his lips over the thought. Because it wasn't just the Vances and Walker who would profit. Every businessman on

Shipwreck would eventually be involved. Why, there wasn't a contractor or politician or labor leader in this part of the state who wouldn't benefit in one way or another—

"You sound like you'd even vote for the god-damned thing," Jonas said. "For Palm Beach Northwest?"

Grayson glanced quickly at him and then shrugged. "Maybe, maybe not, I don't know. There's a lot of hard feeling both ways. But my boss sure would. And he sure changed his interest in this case after Brighton Walker paid him a visit this morning. Duncan, the point is there are *hundreds* of people who might have taken a shot at Wilbur Styles, even if they just *thought* Styles could upset Trevor Vance or his plans in any way."

All right, Jonas impatiently allowed. Maybe so. But last Sunday there certainly weren't any hundreds of people who had ever even heard of Wilbur Styles, let alone who knew of his visit to Starfish Island. Grayson nodded. Grayson's men had pretty well traced those three hours Styles had spent on Shipwreck before the ferry left. And they had found that Styles hardly spoke to anyone. He spent most of the time buried in newspapers in the back booth of a diner. He seemed nervous and fearful of being seen. He was definitely relieved when he could buy his ticket and scamper aboard the ferry to get away from there.

"So we're right back where we started," Jonas said. "Only if nobody followed him, then who could have been over here waiting for him to get off the ferry?"

"A hired killer, for one. Somebody's willing friend, for another."

"It's still a hell of a place to kill anybody," Jonas said. "So it had to be somebody who was pretty desperate. And maybe still is. What about Trevor Vance himself? Did you check out his story?"

"He went out fishing like he told you," Grayson said. "Afterward he was seen in a couple of mainland bars, and then he left to ride with somebody to Seattle. But that was all later on at night. A lot later than he'd implied."

"You mean he could have been here when the ferry docked?"

"It's possible. There are lots of places around here you can tie up an outboard for half an hour without anybody noticing it."

Or an inboard, Jonas suddenly thought, thinking of the sport fisherman, remembering that Lila had been left all alone that night, or so she said.

"Where was Mike Kettenring?" Jonas said. "The big lug who works for them over there?"

"He's got different stories; we're checking them now. But look, anybody could have been here. You can fly from one island to another in five or ten minutes. There are plenty of pilots and charter-boat skippers who'll keep their mouths shut."

"And Brighton Walker has his own plane."

"Sure. And Cynthia Vance has her own license."

"All right. But I don't see either one of them killing Styles in person. And neither do you, or you wouldn't have been so uninterested in that gun of Cynthia's."

Grayson snorted disgustedly. "Don't you understand yet? I've *got* to play it that way. The minute I go pushing on either one of those two, the rug gets pulled out from under me!"

Jonas frowned. "How about Trevor Vance? Doesn't your boss worry about upsetting him? Trevor's still the big applecart over there. Starfish is still mostly in his name, I find."

"Trevor Vance," Grayson said, "is a baby carriage. His wife can wheel him any way she wants. You don't think he could have ever hung onto that property by himself, do you?"

"Well, originally he saved his inheritance with some insurance money he collected on a boat, isn't that right?"

"Oh, it was his money, all right. But not his brains. She's the one who made the parlay, played banks and creditors against each other until land prices started booming. And then she met Walker and he brought some real cash into the business, plus all the big-time tricks of the trade."

"So you think one of them hired a killer, is that it? Just to swat a little fly named Styles who came buzzing around, bothering Trevor Vance?"

"Neither one of them would even think twice. The Dragon Lady, that's what some people call her. And as for Walker—"

"All right, I get the idea," Jonas interrupted sharply. "But I asked you about Mike Kettenring. Has he got a record?"

"Not by name. We haven't checked his prints yet. Why?"

"Just a hunch. But to hire a killer quick you need a contact, don't you?" And then Jonas rapidly told Grayson about his first meeting with Mike and the subsequent fight in the alley with Billy and his friend. Grayson had already heard some of the story from

155

the Vances but it hadn't meant much to him. There were all sorts of stories about Trevor's occasional drunken escapades, but Grayson thought most of them were exaggerated. The couple of times Trevor had got in fights on Shipwreck Island didn't really amount to anything, and in Grayson's opinion Cynthia Vance simply sweat her husband's drinking too much. Though no wonder, with all there was at stake now. Christ, if Trevor should ever chase the wrong politician's wife or take a drunken poke at the wrong newspaper editor—!

Again Jonas interrupted Grayson. "Billy and his friend were GIs of some kind, I'm pretty sure of that. But not from Fort Lewis."

"How do you know?"

"A friend of mine in Seattle did some checking."

"Your friend at the Snoqualmie?"

"That's right. But you could check a lot quicker, both military and civilian sources. It shouldn't be hard to find them. Billy had a badly broken nose."

Grayson nodded and hastily jotted down the expert descriptions which Jonas rattled off. "I can't put out a want without a charge, though," Grayson said. "And I don't see how those guys could tie into this."

"Neither do I," Jonas said. "But I'd like to talk to Billy. And I mean fast. Before the storm hits. And don't ask me which storm because I don't know yet."

"I'll think about it," Grayson said, pocketing his notebook. Grayson suddenly seemed unhappy with the take-charge way Jonas was acting.

"Captain," Jonas said sharply, "how much time have you got before your boss pulls the plug on this investigation?"

"A day or two maybe, unless I can show some-thing."

"Then you'd better get moving, hadn't you?" Jonas opened the car door and a blast of cold wind whipped in. The barometer was falling, all right.

"Listen, Duncan," Grayson said harshly. "The only reason I talked to you at all was because I thought you might dig the spot I'm in and help. But you haven't given me one damn thing."

"So how about this?" Jonas said. "I've been talking on the phone to some insurance men in California. They're checking on that policy Trevor Vance had on his boat once."

"Why?"

"I'll let you know when I find out. But Wilbur Styles sailed on that boat just before Vance bought it. And Styles did some pretty good forging, in his time."

"He passed a lot of bad checks, if that's what you mean."

"Also doctors' prescriptions and a lot of other easy stuff. But at least once he helped another friend col-lect on an insurance fraud, using phony estimates, forged affidavits."

Grayson stared at him. Jonas grinned and took the bottle out of the dash. There wasn't much left in it. "I'll just give the rest of this to Charlie with your compliments, okay?"

And he pocketed the bottle and walked rapidly off toward B Street.

Grayson didn't stop him.

17 The wind was filled with particles of salt spray and sugar-fine sand that blasted his cheeks and tore tears from his eyes. It plastered his pants to his leaden legs as he tried to keep up with a seventy-five-year-old stork who used to practice medicine, and sometimes still did, here on the west coast of Vancouver Island. They were on a lonely beach not far from Tofino, not far from Long Beach, and, on a glowering day like today, not far from the North Pole.

The doctor paused to kick a curved piece of driftwood out of the sand. He tossed it toward harder sand and shouted something to Jonas, then pointed out toward distant rocks and shouted something else which Jonas couldn't hear, and then took off again at his gangling gallop. Jonas took off after him. It wasn't just the wind that was so deafening today, it was the oversize roar of the surf. Those rows and rows of combers out there must reach all the way to Japan.

The doctor scrambled up onto one of the huge driftwood logs which made the logs on Jonas's own shingle seem like matchsticks. The doctor trotted along the log, then jumped down out of sight on the other side, and a moment later Jonas dropped down to join him. They were in a deep hollow, there in the lee of the log with sand dunes bracketing them, and the air was suddenly still, the roar of the surf only a distant freeway rumble.

"You pointed to those rocks back there," Jonas said, "but I couldn't hear you."

"That's where she hit," the doctor said. "Those big rocks are all part of a reef. It runs out several miles toward the little island where the old lighthouse is." Then he gestured toward a couple of silvery planks which stuck out of the sand nearby. "A few days later she washed up here. What was left of her, that is. Any usable lumber has been stripped, of course. Not much more of the hull still buried down there."

Jonas touched the planks. There was nothing to see here. But the doctor must have seen some things in times past. Stafford Lewis, in Victoria, had set up this meeting for Jonas. The doctor and a couple of other elderly locals whom Jonas would meet later were the best authorities on the sinking of Trevor Vance's big sloop, according to Stafford and his RCMP files.

"Doctor, I understand you've done some sailing yourself," Jonas said. "This must have been quite a boat once."

"Oh, quite; yes, battered as she was when I first saw her, she was still a beautiful thing."

"Do you think she was worth a hundred thousand dollars? That was back when the dollar was worth quite a bit more, remember."

The doctor looked up at the gray sky. Drops of rain were starting to skid sideways into the sand around them. "Damned if I know," he said. "We'd better keep moving." And off he trotted again.

They were blown back down the beach, where the

doctor paused to pick up the pieces of driftwood which he had spotted or kicked loose from the sand earlier. He loaded Jonas up with them and carried the heavy ones himself as they trudged up to the place in the woods where the doctor's jeep was parked. By the time they had dumped the driftwood into the back and climbed into the front seat they were both soaking wet.

"My wife makes things out of these," the doctor said. "Makes all sorts of things. I'll show you."

They bounced and slid along a narrow rutted road beneath towering spruce and giant hemlocks until they reached a cleared area and a slightly wider road which at least had some gravel on it. They stopped beside a white picket fence which bravely surrounded a tiny cemetery but was scant defense against the encroaching jungle. Wooden tombstones rotted quickly here, Jonas noticed, but the stone ones often tipped over or sank. The doctor gestured to several markers which were made of driftwood.

"That's some of my wife's doing," he said. "And when you see a well-tended grave, the chances are it's one of my ex-patients. She still works out my guilt for me."

He led Jonas to a clean mound of moss on which there was a simple flat stone bearing the name FRANK BLOODWORTH.

"Was he ever a patient?" Jonas said.

"No, no. Dead several days before the sea calmed down enough so our rescue chaps could even get to his body. The waves had left him high and dry up on one of those rocks out there, near where the boat broke up."

Jonas shivered. The rain was starting to come

down in torrents. "Think this storm will be that bad?"

The doctor smiled. "Scarcely," he said. "That one mowed down three-hundred-foot trees like grass. It sank five fishing craft and a freighter, just between here and Nootka Sound."

"So it wasn't surprising that Vance's sloop went aground? None of the people here blamed it on bad navigation, or bad seamanship, or anything like that?"

The doctor looked sharply at him. "What are you driving at?"

"I don't know yet. But boats that size were hard to sell nine years ago. And that one carried a lot of insurance."

The doctor smiled. "Mr. Duncan, if you weren't a friend of Inspector Lewis, I'd say you were daft. You saw those rocks out there. Is that any place to sink a boat on purpose?" He shook his head and cantered back toward the jeep.

"No, I guess not," Jonas said. "Not unless you were the world's greatest swimmer." Or sailor, he thought. Such a good sailor you'd have to take a chance like that in order to make an accident seem convincing.

"Well, Trevor Vance didn't make it by swimming," the doctor said, as they piled soggily back into the car. "He was just plain lucky. He rode a log in that rolled and nearly killed him when he hit shallow water. And he still wouldn't have made it if a lumberman who lives out that way hadn't seen a fluorescent life jacket floundering around in the surf. It took thirty-eight stitches to tie Vance back together again."

"Vance *was* your patient, then?"

The doctor nodded and put the jeep back into motion. "For over two weeks. Our little hospital was full of sailors off the freighter, so I kept him in my own house. Vance had a pretty rough time of it, half out of his mind over his missing friend and losing the boat and then Bloodworth's sister showing up."

"Cynthia. You mean she was expecting to meet her brother here in Tofino?"

"Close by here. She knew her brother was going to need some more money, even though she'd already sent him five hundred dollars in San Diego, three weeks before."

"That was to pay Vance for smuggling him into Canada."

"Yes, I know about that. Lots of your young men did it and I never blamed them. It was a stupid damn war. Anyway, Bloodworth's sister flew out from Chicago several days after the storm. I wasn't home when she got here, but I guess she damn near took Vance's head off when she discovered her brother was dead. She'd practically raised him, I gathered."

"Doctor," Jonas said, "when you examined Frank Bloodworth's body after it was recovered, was there any indication of a fight? Any indication that he might have been killed?"

The doctor was so startled by the question that he almost ran off the road. "Of course not!" he snorted. "Bloodworth died from exposure and drowning. Didn't even have many contusions or abrasions. But you know what just struck me?" His voice softened curiously. "Bloodworth's sister asked me that same question; she insisted I examine him very carefully. When I said no, he couldn't possibly have been killed, that's when she finally started to cry, started to accept what had happened."

"I wonder what she was expecting?"

"She thought he might have been murdered just for that five hundred dollars. Can you imagine? But that's what Ernie Gore says, and he was our pastor then. He comforted her quite a bit. For years, he says, that poor girl had lived in the fear her brother would die in violence, one way or another. She just couldn't imagine him even knowing anybody who wouldn't steal or lie, someone like Trevor Vance who was just as unhappy as she was about what had happened. But Ernie helped her understand. And she and Vance ended up helping each other, of course. Anyway, Ernie Gore will be at my house; you can ask him yourself. He knows a lot more than I do, and Ernie loves to talk. Now Sydney—that's Sydney Williams, the lumberman who pulled Vance out of the surf—he's different. He'll just sit there puffing on his pipe, so if you want to ask Sydney anything—"

Jonas interrupted before the doctor could wander any further afield. "Did they pull anything else out of the surf," he asked, "or off the wreckage? I'm talking about salvage. On a big boat like that there must have been a lot of valuable instruments and fittings."

"As far as I know," the doctor said, "nobody ever recovered anything worth five cents out there. But don't take my word. That's more in Clarence's department. Clarence was one of our local Mounties at that time, before his arthritis got so bad, and he's the one who would know if anything was stolen or how much the boat was worth or who checked it out for insurance, that sort of thing, so the minute we get to the house we'll get Clarence on the telephone. . . ."

But when they got to the doctor's house there was no chance for Jonas to talk to Clarence or Sydney or Ernie or any other local informant, because the doctor's wife had a message for Jonas to call a long-distance operator. And after several moments of frustration, the call finally got through. Cynthia Vance was on the phone.

The connection was bad and it was hard to understand her, because Cynthia was not only upset but also fearful that Jonas might be on a party or rural line of some sort. She had tracked Jonas down, first through Charlie and then through Inspector Lewis, and she wanted to see him as quickly as possible. She simply had to see him; she would meet him partway in Nanaimo or Victoria or anywhere he liked—

"But what's happened?" Jonas said. "What's wrong?"

And then he suddenly understood what she was desperately trying to say without using the exact words on the telephone:

Trevor Vance had taken off again. Trevor had disappeared.

18 The wheels of the small plane splashed down on the dark runway. In a cloud of spray the plane slowed and turned and rocked like a sea gull toward the rain-swept airport terminal. When they finally stopped, the pilot let out a deep breath, and for the first time in a year Jonas felt a sudden craving for a cigarette. A man's voice whispered, "Can we open our eyes now, Mummy?" and everyone laughed much too loudly.

Jonas ran through the rain to a building where limousines were being loaded with passengers whose flights had been canceled. Even a big jet flight to Sea-Tac had just been grounded. He found an empty space in one of the limousines and a short time later arrived in Victoria.

She was waiting for him outside the automobile entrance of the Empress Hotel. Even under the protection of the porte cochere there was rain blowing hard off the Inner Harbor, and Cynthia looked frozen, despite a fur hat and fur coat which reached to her ankles and made her look even more like a princess. When Jonas got out of the limousine she ran to him and almost hugged him.

"Oh, thank God," she said. "Have you got a bag?"

"A little one."

"Everett will find it. You'll take care of it, won't you, Everett." The busy doorman she spoke to smiled and touched his cap. And then clinging with both hands to one of Jonas's arms she hurried him inside the hotel.

"Your nose is red," Jonas said. "How come you were waiting outside?"

"I've been there for hours, watching every bus, every car, just crossing my fingers. I was scared to death you'd never get farther than Port Alberni."

"I hitchhiked on a lumber company plane," he said, and then stopped to turn her into one of the hotel's bar restaurants. "I need a drink, don't you?"

"Oh, Lord, yes."

"Not to mention something to eat." He glanced at his watch. "You have your car here, right? Well, the last ferry home won't leave for a couple of hours, so there's still time—"

"It won't leave at all tonight," she said. "They're saying Haro Strait looks like the North Sea."

A maitre d' was approaching them with a big smile for Cynthia.

"Hello, Georges," she said quickly. "We don't need a table. But Jonas, what would you like?"

Jonas looked curiously at her before answering. "Well, I was thinking of a double Scotch and one of those thick pieces of rare roast beef. And for that we do need a table. A nice, big, secluded—"

Cynthia interrupted him with a pleading glance. "Oh, but I don't feel like listening to music, do you? Georges, why don't you send us a whole bottle, if you can. Or just several doubles and plenty of ice. I'll have the roast beef, too. Oh, and a bottle of red wine, you know what I like."

"Of course, Mrs. Vance."

"I'd call room service, but you always remember the little things like radishes and a good cheese plate."

"I'll arrange everything, Mrs. Vance," Georges said, and, to Jonas, "The drinks will be up directly, sir, don't worry."

"Thank you, Georges," said Cynthia. She gave him a room number and then moved quickly back into the main corridor with Jonas beside her. "Jonas, we just *can't* talk in there. And as long as we're marooned here anyway . . ." She stopped to fumble in her purse while they walked past elegant shops and through the busy main lobby.

"Marooned," Jonas said. "Well, at least it's my favorite desert island."

But she didn't smile, she wasn't even listening, and then she produced a room key from her purse which she gave to Jonas.

"Here," she said. "This one is yours."

He looked at the number on the key. It was the room next to hers.

They reached the elevators and there was no chance to speak privately until they got off at the seventh floor and walked around a corner toward the front of the hotel. Then Jonas shook his head and smiled. "Cynthia, don't you ever stop running things? Don't you ever stop giving orders?"

He was immediately sorry he'd said it. Her quick glance was that of a child who had been slapped, and

167

she dropped her head while she fumbled in her purse again for another key. When they reached the door to her room her fingers were trembling so badly she couldn't get the key into the lock. Jonas gently took over and opened the door.

The room was a big corner one which looked out toward the Parliament Buildings and the wind-blown Inner Harbor. But Cynthia wasn't looking; she was fumbling with the door chain. "I didn't think you'd mind, Jonas," she whispered shakily. "I'm sorry."

"No, I am," he said, and he took off her coat and sat her down firmly in a chair. "Only don't come apart yet. Just tell me what happened. Any more news of Trevor?"

"No."

"How long has he been gone?"

"Since last night sometime, I guess. Or early this morning. I don't really know."

"Who does know?" Jonas tried to sound as matter-of-fact and impersonal as possible. That wasn't easy, he noticed, if he let himself look at her frightened eyes.

"Well, nobody, exactly. I mean, I spent last night in Whale Harbor. With friends. When I flew home early this morning, Trevor just wasn't there."

"Who was?"

"I don't know. I mean—Lila, of course. But I got home quite early and woke her up. She didn't know anything was wrong. She said maybe Trevor just went out for a walk."

"So then what did you do?"

"Well, I called Mr. Bakewell first, I think. But he

couldn't find him and nobody could find him and then someone noticed the boat was gone, that same one Trevor took the time before, the big outboard he likes to go fishing in sometimes when he doesn't want to bother with the sport fisherman. So I sent Mike over to the mainland. He's been checking his usual contacts, Trevor's favorite bars and all."

"And Lila's still at the house?"

"Yes, she's telephoning everyplace she can think of."

"How about Brig Walker? What's he doing to help?"

"Well, he had to move his floatplane back to Seattle early this morning, after he dropped me off at Shipwreck. That's where I'd left my car."

"You mean Brig was with you in Whale Harbor last night?"

"Oh, not in the same room or anything, if that's what you think. We stayed at the Iversons'. There was a meeting of realtors we just couldn't postpone. But anyway, when Brig heard the storm warnings, early this morning, he thought his plane would be safer if he moored it back in Seattle."

"So he left you before you knew Trevor was missing?"

"Yes, but I reached Brig later by phone, of course. He said he'd check everywhere *he* could think of, and he told me not to worry, not yet anyway, not until we'd covered all the usual bars and places."

"Told you not to worry!" Jonas snorted. "Your husband takes off in a boat, and a few hours later some bad weather turns into practically a hurricane—"

"But the sound was relatively quiet last night and

this morning! There was plenty of time for Trevor to get safely to the mainland, or anywhere else. That's true, Jonas!"

"All right. But was it also Brig Walker who made you so worried the police might find out about this?"

"No. Well, maybe a little. Anyway, it was Brig who insisted I call the Coast Guard."

"And did you?"

She nodded a bit weakly. "Just before I finally reached you in Tofino, I . . . I called them to report the boat missing."

"*Boat* missing. Jesus H. Christ!"

Cynthia almost cringed at the anger in his voice. At that moment there was a knock on the door. It was a waiter bearing liquor and glasses and ice. Jonas told him to go right back and bring up the food, too. He shut the door and poured a stiff drink and put it into Cynthia's shaking hand.

"Drink this," he said. "Drink the whole damn thing," and she nodded and did her best to obey him.

By the time the food arrived a few moments later, Cynthia was already calmer. Under Jonas's questioning she filled in the rest of what had happened, or what she knew had happened. He also made her eat while she talked, for she obviously hadn't eaten anything all day.

The sequence was clear enough. Apparently Trevor Vance had passed out in the middle of the afternoon yesterday, which certainly wasn't surprising, considering the condition he was in when Jonas had last seen him, just before Jonas left Starfish Island. Mike had put Trevor to bed; then, thinking that Trevor would surely sleep the clock around, Mike went into town on Shipwreck to do some more partying of his own. He also went bowling and ended up in an all-night poker game, or so he told Cynthia when he showed up at home this morning.

"Big help, isn't he," Jonas said. "Obeys like a dog."

"I guess I can't blame Mike," Cynthia said. "I'm the one who shouldn't have stayed away all night."

"But Lila didn't, did she?"

No, Lila had spent yesterday afternoon in a beauty parlor, then went to dinner and a movie with a girl friend. Lila came back from Shipwreck shortly before midnight. That was confirmed by Mr. Bakewell, whom Lila had stopped to see for a few minutes when she noticed his lights were still on. But the trouble was, neither one of them knew that Mike had left Trevor all alone in the big house. And so Lila, as she often did, sneaked in the back way and up to her rooms, which were in the rear wing of the house. There she locked her door and went to sleep. She had simply assumed that Trevor and Mike were still at their carousing, and even if they weren't she certainly had no desire to see either one of them. Not after something that had happened yesterday which Lila refused to tell Cynthia about.

"Mike tried to rape her," Jonas said.

"Mike—what?" Cynthia gasped. But then something about it made her giggle, too, and she reached for the wine bottle. Jonas reached for it quicker—she had obviously had enough to drink—and for a second their hands fought over the bottle as Cynthia's giggle turned into laughter. But then the telephone rang and she jumped to her feet so fast the wine spilled onto her dress. By the time Jonas had caught and steadied the bottle, Cynthia had already grabbed up the telephone.

"Yes? Hello?" And then she gasped, "Oh, yes, it's about time! Put her through! Quick!"

It was Lila and the connection was very bad. So was her news, or absence of it. There was no word of Trevor yet, not from Mike or Walker or Bakewell or anyone else who was discreetly searching, and there was nothing from the Coast Guard either. Cynthia nodded helplessly—she looked shaky again—so Jonas took the phone out of her hand.

But there was little more he could learn from Lila, except that the reason she hadn't called earlier was because the telephone lines to the big house were out and she had had to make her way through the storm to Bakewell's cottage, where she had just been phoning to check with everyone, and that's where she was now. Quite a number of trees on Starfish had already been blown down, and Bakewell's TV aerial had just been ripped off the roof. "Oh, Jonas," Lila squealed, "it's so exciting! It's the most exciting storm I ever saw!" Lila sounded like a little kid.

Jonas hung up. Cynthia was looking at him in white-faced panic. All effects of the liquor had disappeared. "What are we going to do?" she whispered.

"Nothing," Jonas said matter-of-factly. "There's nothing we can do, except turn this over to the only people who might be able to find him. Whether you and Brig Walker are afraid of the publicity or not."

He picked up the phone again and put in a call for Captain Grayson. Cynthia watched anxiously but she didn't object or try to interfere. And when the call got through to a sergeant who was manning Grayson's office, Cynthia asked to speak to him herself. She calmly and steadily told the sergeant what had happened. She hoped that he understood the urgency of her concern; yes, the sergeant already realized this was no simple Missing Person case. He was sure that Grayson would order an immediate full-scale search for Trevor Vance.

Cynthia hung up the phone and quietly started to cry. Jonas put a quick arm around her to help her to a couch, where she clung exhaustedly to him. When her sobbing eased a bit, Jonas said gently, "Cynthia, what is it you're so afraid of? That he may have killed a man, that he may be running away? That he might kill himself? Or that *he* might be the one who's in danger—?"

"No, no, no, stop it," she begged. "I just don't know, Jonas! I don't! Please, can't you just . . . just hold me?"

He held her then, held her close until her crying came to a final stop and she lay quietly against him. He could feel her heart beating.

"Jonas," she said, "what happened to her? To Kathy?"

Jonas grunted, startled. "What? Oh, that was over three years ago. It was on Olympic Boulevard. This damn junkie in a stolen car came through a red light going ninety miles an hour—" He checked himself awkwardly and then suddenly started to disentangle himself to rise from the couch.

But Cynthia stopped him. "I'm sorry," she said quickly, still clinging to him. "I won't ask any more." Then after another long moment she said, even more quietly, "Jonas, do you know that a starfish can turn its stomach inside out? It can stick its stomach right out of its body to wrap around things or work its way right into the shell of a clam or a mussel, and pretty quick there just isn't any more clam or mussel."

"No," Jonas said, "I didn't know that."

Her voice was trembling again. "Nobody suspects. They're such pretty things, shaped just like Christmas stars and with all those lovely colors. . . . But Jonas, that's what happened to Trevor, to make him drink more and more. That's what happened to both of us. We should have just sold Starfish for the land, three or four years ago, and got out of there. We could have, and still made enough money. We could have escaped before it got such a grip on us with all those hundreds of clinging little suckers, until now it's too late, until now that greedy big stomach is tearing him apart and eating us both up. . . ."

She stopped, and Jonas thought for a minute that she was crying again. But after a couple of deep breaths to control herself, she suddenly giggled.

"I can feel your stomach," she said, and glanced down. "Oh, Lord, I spilled wine on my dress, didn't I. And now it's getting on your shirt." With a quick twist she reached behind her and pulled the zipper of her dress and wriggled it down over her shoulders all in the same movement. She gave the skirt a downward tug and a kick and the whole dress landed on the floor. "There," she said, as she snuggled back close to him.

A warning flash of no, this isn't right! went through Jonas's brain, all mixed up with desire and panic and reasons why not, with She's just scared and we're in a public hotel and I'm an older man than she thinks

I am and it just can't be like this. But her slip was thin and slippery under his hands, and he could feel the warmth of her soft skin beneath it. He could feel her heart beating again, beating against his chest, beating harder now. He could feel his own heart beating twice as fast and hard. He could feel the tightness in his trousers, feel the swelling of an erection.

Of its own unthinking accord, his nose nudged her cheek and suddenly he was kissing her and she was hungrily kissing him back.

It wasn't until a long time later, when she slept peacefully in his arms while the storm sucked and blew at the windows outside, that a startling realization crept sleepily through Jonas's last consciousness:

Cynthia Vance was almost as rusty as he was.

19 When he woke up the next morning she was gone.

He remembered that sometime during the night he had moved into his own next-door room, for the sake of the usual proprieties in a hotel where Cynthia was well known and liked, and when he left her she murmured something about his coming back for breakfast. The connecting door between their rooms had been unlocked then. But now, at seven thirty in the morning, only his side of the door was open. Hers was locked. And by the time he had hurried through a stinging shower and lightning shave and into his clothes, by the time he had opened the drapes to spots of early sunshine and fleeing clouds, by the time he left his room to stroll casually along the corridor, he saw that maids were already moving in and out of the other room. Cynthia was not only gone, she was gone for good.

Jonas hadn't slept as late as seven thirty for a long time, and for some silly reason he felt guilty about it. He hurried downstairs, where guests were already milling in front of cashiers' windows and airline desks. At the main desk the clerks were even busier, so he went straight out to the side automobile entrance. There he hastily described Cynthia's car to a busy doorman, who nodded even before Jonas could finish his description. The obviously well-tipped doorman said Cynthia had left over half an hour ago. Extra ferries were being put on to handle the congestion from yesterday's and last night's cancellations. Cynthia wanted to be as far up in the waiting line at Sidney as possible, so she wouldn't miss the first ferry home.

Jonas hesitated, wanting to ask another question or two, but he didn't want to seem overly curious so he nodded to the doorman and walked briskly down the drive toward Government Street. The morning was biting cold but it was the cold of spring again. That sneaky last storm of winter was already being chased away and, though flags still whipped in the wind, there were private boats leaving their moorings across the street; though whitecaps danced on the water of the Inner Harbor, there was already a commercial floatplane taxiing out for its takeoff to Vancouver.

Jonas turned left and hurried across the street to Thunderbird Park. He walked as fast as he could and it felt wonderful. The cold air burned his lungs and that felt even better. He waved to one of the huge totem poles which reminded him of one of Charlie's. He walked around a lamppost twice just to soak in the clear clear blue of the lobelia in the hanging baskets overhead. He suddenly remembered how good he had felt in that fight in the alley in Seattle when he landed a couple of hard blows he didn't know he could still manage.

177

But the memory made him laugh at himself and he felt foolish and guilty again. What the hell was he doing out here, anyway? What the hell was he doing last night?

Jonas walked back to the hotel and put in a call to Captain Grayson, who would call him back just as soon as he could be reached, they said. The captain had probably been up all night.

Jonas stopped at the main desk and asked that his bill be made up, but the clerk asked him to wait a moment and then came back with the news that there were no charges. Jonas's room had already been paid for by Mrs. Trevor Vance. Jonas didn't know whether to feel embarrassed or angry. Only why should he feel either? In a way, he was working for her, wasn't he? And then the clerk handed him an envelope which had been left in his box. Jonas nodded his thanks and moved away. As he walked toward the downstairs coffee shop he tore open the envelope and unfolded a piece of hotel stationery. At least she hadn't left him a check this time. But then he read the short message. *Thank you,* it said. *I am sure she would forgive you.* It was signed simply: *C.*

He read it again and smiled and relaxed. Oh, Kathy, Kathy, he thought, am I still so transparent? He ate half a breakfast, answered the page for his phone call, and went back to work.

Trevor Vance was still missing, Grayson said. There wasn't a single clue to his whereabouts, and the way the captain felt this morning he wasn't sure he gave a damn. To hear Grayson tell it on the phone, that storm must have landed right on top of the sheriff's office. But don't worry, despite all their other problems a full search was under way for Vance, not only in the sound area but all over the state and in BC, too. Early this morning Grayson thought they might have a lead when King County reported locating that serviceman named Billy. Billy was an enlisted man in Naval Support, it seemed, as was his buddy, who unfortunately was out of town on a pass. But apparently Billy didn't know a damned thing about Trevor Vance, he hadn't even known his name —though when Billy was shown a photograph, he did admit that he had seen Vance several days ago in a sleazy Seattle bar. And, sure, he might have had a little quarrel with him. But that's about all Billy would admit or remember and there wasn't much point in pushing him; he couldn't know much more, let alone know anything about Vance's present whereabouts, because after Billy got his nose broken he went straight back to his base at Sand Point, where he had been ever since, most of the time in sick bay.

"Where is he now?" Jonas asked.

"County courthouse in Seattle," Grayson said. "But they just brought him into the sheriff's office for questioning, that's all. There's nothing to hold him on. Not unless you want to prefer charges for assault and make a real mess out of everything. But Trevor Vance told me *he* sure wouldn't make any complaint, the other day."

"Neither would I," Jonas said.

"That's what I figured. Why pick on a sailor? This Billy guy can't help us, Duncan. Forget him."

"No, I won't," Jonas said suddenly, firmly. "Not for a couple of hours at least. Couldn't they hang onto him there for just a couple of more hours?"

They could. And so two hours and twenty minutes

later, when Billy walked alone out of the county courthouse building in Seattle, he was startled to see a man waiting for him on the sidewalk. The man grinned at the big bandage which still decorated Billy's nose. "Hello, Billy," the man said. "My name is Jonas Duncan. Remember me?"

Billy licked his lips. Of course he remembered, and furthermore he now knew who Jonas Duncan was. They had just told him, back inside there. What the hell was going on, anyway? Billy answered warily, stiffly. "Yes, sir," he said. "What do you want, sir?"

"Just talk a little," Jonas said pleasantly, "that's all. Mind if I walk along with you?"

"I've got to get back to the base," Billy said, not moving. "They kept me a lot longer than they said they would."

"Well, I wouldn't worry," Jonas said. "Say, it's funny, isn't it, the way an injury to your nose blackens both of your eyes, too? I remember once when I was a cop—"

"Look, Mr. Duncan," Billy interrupted sharply, "a friend of mine in Shore Patrol said if I came down here voluntarily I wouldn't have to answer any questions I didn't want to. And those sheriff's guys were nice about it, they didn't crowd me, they said all they cared about was trying to locate this guy named Trevor Vance."

"Oh, I don't want you to incriminate yourself either," Jonas said. "I won't ask a lot of questions."

"Well, I'm sorry if I hit you in that alley, sir."

"Forget it."

Billy was relaxing but only a little. "Anyway, I really should be catching a bus, now."

"Okay," Jonas said. "I'll just walk over to the bus stop with you."

There was no way out of it for Billy. They moved along the sidewalk together.

"This Trevor Vance they're looking for is a pretty important man," Jonas said after a moment. "I guess they told you that, too?"

"Yes, sir," Billy said. "They told me. But I said there's no way I can help. *I* don't know anything about him. He was just another guy in a bar. And me, I was so drunk I didn't remember much, anyway."

Jonas nodded understandingly. "You mean, you didn't mention the other stuff, whatever it was."

"The what?" Billy said, startled.

"Well, let's not kid each other." Jonas laughed. "You were sky high on something besides booze, that day."

Billy flushed angrily. "Oh, no, you don't, mister! You're not going to hang any drug thing on me!"

"Now, don't worry. I'd rather not even mention it to anybody. I know how the Navy is about things like that." Jonas nodded to Billy's uniform sleeve. "Particularly if a man has a good rating like yours. I'd hate to have you lose any of those stripes."

Billy glared at him, then suddenly took hold of Jonas's arm, and they turned out of the sidewalk traffic into the seclusion of a building alcove.

"All right," Billy said grimly, "what do you want?"

"The truth about something," Jonas said quietly. He already felt like a heel for the way he was handling the sailor. But there was one shot in the dark which he simply had to take, even though he knew it might make him feel a lot worse.

181

"Well, go on," Billy said.

Jonas spoke quietly. "Back there in the sheriff's office, did anybody suggest that you and Trevor Vance had tangled over a girl?"

Billy hesitated a moment. "I guess somebody must have told them something like that. Yeah. I suppose it could have been true, but I sure didn't remember knowing any girls in that place, so I don't really know what they were talking about. A fight's a fight, that's all. I told you I was sorry."

"Sure," Jonas said. "And they've probably already checked with the bartenders. Maybe there weren't even any girls there." Jonas took a breath. "So here's what I want to know: What was his name?"

"Huh?"

"Your girl friend. Tell me about him."

For a second Jonas thought Billy was going to slug him, right there in public. But Billy was far too scared for that. "Why, you son of a bitch," he blustered, "have you ever got things backwards! Call me one, will you?"

"Then straighten it out, sailor. Fast!"

Billy looked wildly around, but there was no help anywhere. "Look," he said, "I haven't told anybody. Neither has my buddy. He's out of town visiting his mother; she's sick. But maybe you noticed, he's not as big as I am. He's not as big as your friend Vance, either."

"Go on," Jonas said harshly. "What happened?"

"Well, there was this other place up the street called the Green Garter. And my buddy went into the men's room, that's all, to take a piss. This Vance, he follows him. And he takes one look and he hauls out a five-dollar bill and says, 'Sailor, I'll give you five dollars—' Oh, shit, you know what I'm talking about! When my buddy told him to bug off, Vance tried to grab him. Only then I walked in and Vance took off like a ruptured rabbit. We split and went after him. I finally flushed him out of that other joint—hell, you know the rest."

Jonas nodded slowly. "Yes," he said, "I guess so. Only why were you so afraid to tell it? Why haven't you told anyone else?"

Billy snorted righteously. "Because to me, gay is not beautiful, see? You think a guy can lose his stripes fast over drugs? Hah! These days, you can't even call a fairy a queer. That's how I lost my rating once before, just because sometimes when I get high— well, it happens, that's all. I go beat up on some fucking faggot like Trevor Vance!"

20

Brighton Walker stared at Jonas. "I don't believe it," Walker finally said.

Jonas looked out the window. For some reason it was easier to hear what Walker was saying if you didn't watch his face. Besides, the Seattle sky was clearing and the mountain was out. Not that phony pop-art mountain which Walker displayed on rainy days, either. This was the real Rainier, the great white mother of mountains, so big and close it almost scared you to realize she'd been lying there hidden all the time, watching over the whole Northwest from behind her mists and blizzards.

"I don't believe it for one damn minute!" Walker said even more firmly. "That sailor is just trying to make you forget what *he* did."

"Like threatening to cut off my balls, you mean? No," Jonas said, "I should have guessed the truth right then. I probably would have, if you hadn't made Cynthia Vance's story sound so convincing, about her husband stealing the sailor's girl."

"Well, it was true! It must have been. For Christ's sake, Trevor Vance always goes whoring around when he's drunk. Everybody knows that."

"Why? Because you say so? Or because Cynthia Vance does. Which one of you is the liar?"

Walker flushed and rose to step around from behind his desk. "What kind of a crack is that? Duncan, I ought to throw you out of here."

"Yes, but you'd need help for that," Jonas said, "and I notice your boy Terrence isn't around today. Why not? Where is he?"

"I sent him out on his bike to look for Vance in some of the highway spots. What's wrong with that? Duncan, what the hell is wrong with *you?*"

It wasn't a bad question, Jonas suddenly thought.

"What's eating you?" Walker was saying. "Why are you so uptight? Just because some ignorant sadistic jerk called Vance a fairy?"

But he wasn't only uptight, Jonas thought, he was a little sick at his stomach. He took a deep breath. "Okay," he said, "I'll slow down a little. But the other day in that alley, you must have known the real reason why Cynthia did a dumb thing like writing me that check and then just leaving me there flat. She did it because she was desperate and terrified, right? Terrified that Trevor was in such a mess he'd start blabbing to me, to any stranger. He'd just spill out what *really* had happened and lay himself wide open to a morals charge, maybe?"

"Well, he certainly didn't say anything in the car like that. Not while I was with them."

"Oh, but then they dumped you off too, just as fast as they could. Isn't that what you told me?"

"Yes, I guess so." Walker was beginning to look a little uneasy.

"And how many other times has he got in trouble and been spirited away to his island to sober up and fly straight again? And all this macho talk—even Mike Kettenring smirks when he says it, but maybe Mike is one himself, who knows; his wife practically said so. Walker, don't tell me *you* haven't noticed any of the dozen little things that I have."

"All right!" Walker said. "So maybe I have wondered a little, now and then. But it's only been during the last few years, since Trevor started this heavy drinking. And if some latent homosexuality pops out occasionally, so what? There are a lot of closet queens." And then Walker laughed. "Jesus Christ, Duncan, I thought you came from Los Angeles!"

"Sure," Jonas said. "I even put in a couple of years on a vice squad."

"Well, then, don't be so shocked! You must have some understanding, some sympathy for a poor oversexed slob who maybe starts branching out a little when he gets plastered."

"Who said he was oversexed? Cynthia? Has that been her complaint to you? Is that why she needs your friendly compassion now and then?"

Walker's smile ended abruptly. "I don't think that's any of your damned business," he said.

"I wish it weren't," Jonas said harshly. "And I've got plenty of sympathy and understanding, don't worry. But right now they're for only one person. For just Trevor Vance, that's all. Nobody else."

"So what do you want from me?"

"The truth, for once. I know how badly Trevor Vance has been coming apart; I've seen it for myself. But I'm also sure you know a hell of a lot more about it than you've admitted. So how about going back to the courthouse with me, to at least explain some of

186

his sex problem. There's a sheriff's lieutenant there who's in touch with Captain Grayson—"

"Do *what?*" Walker's mouth practically fell open.

"Don't you understand? You said you wanted answers. Well, Trevor Vance may be the only one who has those answers. And now the police are trying to help us find him. But you and Trevor's wife have withheld the one clue that might help locate him in a hurry. If he's a deviate, that changes the whole code of a search. They ought to be hitting the gay bars, checking on current complaints of flashing, molesting—"

"But he doesn't do horrible things like that! My God, Duncan, of course I'm not going to go telling the police—"

"You mean, you're afraid it might get in the newspapers. And the sound area is *not* Los Angeles. And with all the trouble you're having already with your plans for Starfish—"

"Well, you know yourself that some people are more square than others."

"Sure, and you said I was shocked. But do you know what shocks me? The growing thought that maybe you don't even *want* Trevor Vance to be found!"

"That's a lie!"

"Washington is a community property state, right? And Cynthia already has Trevor's power of attorney. So wouldn't it be nice if he just *stayed* lost until you got this whole development deal all signed and sealed and delivered—"

"Why, you lousy bastard," Walker said. "You say one word like that to the police and you're fired!"

"Oh, of course I won't," Jonas said. "Not yet. But maybe the only reason you wanted to hire me in the first place was to spy on the police, to keep you posted—the same way you use Terrence Fall to keep an eye on the people on Starfish."

"I do not! Duncan, you *are* fired! Now, get out of here!"

"I never took the job," Jonas said, "but I'll send you a bill." And he walked out.

He steamed all the way down thirty floors in the elevator. He was still mad when he reached the sidewalk, where he hesitated. But at least some of the sailor's claim about Trevor Vance did have to be reported, and so he turned north to walk back toward the courthouse. It was far too beautiful a day to do anything but walk. The wind that had followed the cold front and washed the sky was now swinging signs and tossing skirts. The sun bounced down off freshly polished glass and concrete. It was the cleanest day in Seattle Jonas could remember, and what the hell was he so mad about, anyway? Why did he take so much out on Brig Walker like that?

Yes, whom was he really mad at? Cynthia, for not ever being quite honest? Cynthia, for using him, perhaps in ways he hadn't even guessed yet? Cynthia, for touching him in a place inside where he didn't want to be touched?

Jonas walked across a street which dropped downhill into Puget Sound, where there were whitecaps in every direction. Bainbridge Island looked so close you could skip a rock across to it, and over it, and after that the rock would dance from one unseen patch of blue to the next until it buried itself in the

188

sparkling snow of the Olympics, fifty miles away on the map but surely no more than five or ten today.

Jonas slowed down. This was the kind of a day when he could be watching porpoises play from his own front porch, and yet here he was on his way to a sheriff's office to alert another sheriff's office, to start teletypes and radios roaring. It was a day when he could be painting a seascape in the happiest colors there were, and yet here he was on his way to turn the black and whites loose on a man who maybe was completely innocent of everything up to and including murder, who maybe only wanted to be alone and left alone, and yet who from now on might be sought and pursued and harassed as a homosexual.

Jonas saw a bench in front of a bank and sat down on it. Just because he was angry was no reason to go leaping with the pack like any other killer whale. He wasn't a cop any more, for God's sake. He didn't have to make any report yet, even in the watered-down version he was thinking of.

But was it safe not to? Jonas shivered. It was really himself he was mad at. He knew that. Mad for a lot of things, but mostly for not knowing yet who murdered Wilbur Styles. Maybe Trevor Vance knew and maybe he didn't. But that wasn't the only reason why it was so important to locate Trevor and do it in a hurry. Way down inside, Jonas also wanted somehow to save that poor sad son of a bitch. But how could he help him if he couldn't find him? What if no one ever found him?

Jonas needn't have worried about that, not on so beautiful a day. Because after such a storm as yesterday's, every beach on the islands was dotted with hardy beachcombers braving the icy waters and slippery rolling rocks of high tide. Today all sorts of prizes would be found, from bits of broken boats to whole cases of beer. From farther out would come lost fishing gear and the occasional glass floats which made it through the straits to these partially protected shores.

And even as Jonas sat stewing in Seattle, one joyful woman spotted such a float rolling back and forth with the surge of waves on a distant, pebbly shingle. She stumbled toward the collector's item as fast as her clumsy rubber boots would allow. It wasn't a clear glass ball, like the Japanese floats, but it was just as big, perhaps a Russian one made of plastic, though she couldn't tell yet because it was apparently covered with a webbing of hemp which was soggy with bits of seaweed.

The woman reached for it as another wave rolled it toward her knees. She lifted it into the air and suddenly realized that what she was holding was not hemp but human hair. She started to scream as some of the hair came out. It was streaked with white.

She was holding a severed human head, the head of Trevor Vance.

21 Vance's boat,
the big outboard, was found the next day, not by the
Coast Guard but by a commercial fisherman from
Anacortes who bumped into the half-sunken wreck
and bent his own propeller in the process. When the
outboard was towed in and examined, its motor was
found to be still in forward gear and its throttle still
twisted to what would have been about half speed.
Its hull was upside down and badly battered. There
was a hole in the bottom and one side was partially
caved in, either by a crash into rocks or a collision
with another boat or floating log. Trevor's outboard
showed all the typical damage of a dozen such vic-
tims of the storm. But whatever occupants there had
been in the other sinking boats had somehow
managed to survive. At least so far, Trevor Vance was
the storm's only known human victim.

"The storm's victim? Baloney," Jonas said. He was
talking on the telephone to Sergeant Bill Carruthers,
who had just called him at home to give him the news
of the boat.

"I know," Bill said, "but that's the statement
they're putting out. That's all they're saying."

"So the newspapers will start guessing his head maybe got cut off by the propeller of some freighter, I suppose."

"Look, you're a lot closer to this case than I am," said Bill, "but I suppose it is possible some big white shark took a chomp on Vance's body."

"Or a whole pack of smaller sharks? Not without leaving their calling cards. Not according to Dan Sturdevant. The whites have several rows of slanted teeth that would leave very distinctive marks. And killer whales are distinctive, too. They have bigger, longer, pointed teeth, spaced farther apart."

"Yeah, well, I'm trying to eat a hamburger right now, Jonas. I just thought you'd like to know about the boat."

"Wait a minute," Jonas said. "What's the medical examiner saying? He must have called in all kinds of experts by now to look at that head. At least they must know whether it was lopped off a dead body, like you just implied, or whether it was chopped off when Vance was still alive."

"Christ, call Captain Grayson for that kind of stuff, will you?"

"I tried to but he seems very busy today."

"Well, so am I, Jonas. And now my coffee is getting cold."

"Okay, Bill." Jonas sighed. "Enjoy your hamburger. Thanks."

He hung up and glanced at his watch. It was almost three o'clock and maybe not too soon to try to reach Cynthia Vance again. After flying back from Seattle this morning, Jonas had tried to call the house on Starfish but got no answer, even though the phone company insisted that service had been reinstalled yesterday afternoon. He tried Mr. Bakewell's number but Bakewell didn't answer, either. Then finally, a little after noon, Jonas reached Lila Kettenring. Lila had just come back home alone from the county seat, where they had all gone together early this morning on the sport fisherman, to make statements for Captain Grayson. Lila still sounded badly shaken by what had happened but she was glad to talk to Jonas and tell him what little she knew.

Grayson himself had come out to Starfish last night, apparently, to bring the awful news of that grisly discovery on the beach. He had also brought a couple of men who looked around briefly and noted the place where the missing boat had been moored. Grayson had asked a few questions, but everyone was so shocked that their answers must have made no sense at all, Lila said.

This morning, however, Brig Walker flew over to help, and Cynthia only lost her cool once and nearly fainted when Captain Grayson asked her if she'd like to confirm the identification of her husband's head. Lila offered to do it for her, though Walker angrily insisted this was all nonsense and quite unnecessary and he called in a local lawyer to prove it. But Lila had already looked at the head by then, trying to tell herself it wasn't much worse than looking at a dead fish. And of course it was really Trevor Vance, all right. Several of the sheriff's men knew him, and they agreed there was no question about the identification, so why Captain Grayson wanted to stage that gruesome bit of melodrama Lila had no idea. But someday she'd get even with the stupid bastard, oh, would she ever!

"What's the matter with him, Jonas? Does he think that Trevor was *murdered?* Does he think one of *us* might have cut Trevor's head off?" Lila's voice was beginning to sound a little hysterical.

"I don't know what Grayson thinks," Jonas said quickly. "But where is Cynthia now? I'd like to talk with her."

"Oh, I wish you would. She needs somebody, Jonas. I mean somebody who doesn't *want* something all the time." Lila suddenly giggled a high little giggle. "I guess that's my problem, too. Do you know one of those deputies actually tried to pat my bottom while I was vomiting in his wastebasket?"

"Take it easy, Lila. Pour yourself a drink. Where is she?"

"Oh, I'm sorry," Lila said. "After it was all over, Mike took her to a doctor's office and the doctor gave her something; he wanted her to lie down for a while. So Mike is still over there waiting for her. He'll bring her home on the afternoon ferry, I guess. Anyway, I brought the boat home, so I could do some shopping, like Mrs. Vance wanted. And Brig Walker is busy somewhere with lawyers, at least he was. But I'll have Mrs. Vance call you the minute she comes back or the minute I hear from her. I've got your number, I think—"

"I just gave it to you."

"Oh, yes, here it is. And she won't be longer than two or three hours, I'm sure, so if you'll be there—"

"I'll be here. Drink that drink."

"Oh, thank you. I mean, it's so silly, isn't it? *Me* being scared like this? But I am—oh, God, I'm scared —and I don't even know why!" She hung up abruptly.

That had been two and a half hours ago. Jonas poked impatiently at the fire in the Franklin stove. He walked out to the kitchen to get a can of beer. He was opening it when the phone rang. He turned so quickly that the beer foamed all over his hand. He dropped the can in the sink and hurried back to grab up the ringing telephone.

But it wasn't Cynthia. It was a person-to-person call from Los Angeles, from one of the insurance investigators whom Jonas had been prodding at regular intervals for the past several days. The man finally had some answers for Jonas concerning that hundred-thousand-dollar policy on the sloop. "That's what I've been waiting for," Jonas said, and he grabbed a pencil and pad to scribble notes while the man rattled off his report. It was very complete, a final report, and when he was through Jonas thanked the man and hung up.

Jonas stared at his notes for a long moment, then grimly dialed the local sheriff's substation, in Whale Harbor, and asked to be put through to Captain Grayson on a police line, no matter where Grayson was or what he was doing. And this time, damn it, Jonas didn't want any double-talk—but the operator had already caught the urgency in his voice, and in less than two minutes Grayson himself came on the line. Grayson was in his own office in the county seat, trying to hurry up the lab report on Vance's boat so he could go over the whole case with his boss, and he didn't have much time to talk. But he listened attentively while Jonas rattled off at least the first third of the report.

And then Grayson interrupted. "So it was a bummer, you mean. You got nowhere."

"Well they found the man who made the original appraisal of the sloop in Oakland—the surveyor, they call them—and he says it definitely wasn't overinsured. There were all sorts of instruments and power assists for single handling that actually made it worth even more than one hundred thousand dollars."

"I understand."

"And the investigator who checked the wreckage later on—he's dead now but they finally located all of his notes—he indicated that the sloop hadn't been stripped before sinking or anything like that. There was just no question but that the full insurance should be paid to Vance."

"I read you!"

"They also checked for any possible forgery in any of the files—"

"Yes! That's great! So now we can cross off insurance. That wasn't the favor Styles did for Vance once, so the threat of blackmail was over something else, that's all."

"Wait a minute," Jonas said sharply. "I told you it didn't make any sense for Wilbur Styles to be a blackmailer, remember? In his position he couldn't afford to be. So even though Styles probably knew something—"

"Well, I'll worry about that, Duncan," Grayson said crisply. "But I do appreciate your running this down for me. Oh, and thanks for your message last night on the homo angle, but Brighton Walker had already given my boss a call on the same subject."

"You're kidding."

"Oh, he's some wily bastard, that Walker. He called to offer his help the minute he heard Vance was dead. And the Dragon Lady, she's just as slick, playing the poor bereaved widow."

"Was that why you pulled that silly chamber-of-horrors stunt this morning?"

There was a second of dead silence on the telephone. "Who told you about that?" Grayson asked.

"The girl who threw up instead of Cynthia."

Grayson's voice was coldly correct. "Well, how I get people to spit out the truth is my business, Duncan. But from now on, I'd appreciate your not talking to any of those people over there on Starfish Island."

Jonas laughed. "Oh, captain, relax. I know you've got your boss on your neck, but—"

"No," Grayson interrupted, "no, I don't. This is a whole new ball game, my friend. I've got carte blanche, now. The murder of Trevor Vance is the biggest thing that ever hit this county, and my boss knows it. He could ride all the way to Olympia on this case."

"Well, at least you're calling it murder," said Jonas. "What was the weapon, can the doctors tell yet?"

"That's the trouble," Grayson said. "They can't be sure; we can't *prove* murder yet. But my boss is convinced. That's all I care about." Grayson was brusque and impatient again. "Anyway, I do appreciate what you've done, Duncan. I mean it. But we've got all the help we need over here, and we don't want to make any mistakes on a big one like this. We're going to just take our time and—"

"So there's a mistake, right there," Jonas interrupted sharply. "I told you before, whoever shot Styles had to be pretty desperate. Now Vance's murder shows signs of even more desperation—"

"Oh, yes, sir! Yes, inspector!" Grayson snapped. But then he laughed, not unkindly. "Christ, Jonas, I know how you feel. But get out of the harness, will you? You're retired, remember? I know how hard that must be to get used to, particularly when you're not *quite* that old yet. I know how my own father used to grump around the house. But screw that," he said, running out of empathy. "I'm busier'n hell, Duncan, so I've got to hang up. But I meant what I said. From now on, you just draw pictures or something. Stay out of this case, okay?"

And Grayson hung up.

Jonas put down his own telephone and walked slowly to the fireplace, where there was no fire burning, and deliberately kicked a log just as hard as he dared. His toe hurt like hell but he smiled up at the portrait over the mantel. "See? I'm learning."

Only then the phone rang and he whirled to grab it and he practically roared into it. "Yeah?"

For a second there was only silence marred by the sound of static interference. Finally a frightened female voice whispered, "Mr. Duncan? Is that you?"

It was Lila again. She was on ship–shore phone and the transmission wasn't very good, even though she was so close that Jonas could probably see her boat if he'd look out his window, she said. That is, if his place was the cottage with the red shutters about half a mile south of the pier where his trawler was moored. It was. But Lila was almost frantic because Jonas's line had been busy for so long. The reason she whispered was because Mike was with her, and he was acting sort of funny; he was down in the cabin at the moment—and then there was a burst of static and the connection was broken entirely.

Jonas dropped the phone, grabbed his jacket and his field glasses, and hurried outside. It took only a second to locate the sport fisherman, which was moving quite slowly. It was maybe a half mile offshore and closer to Mrs. Kelly's, actually, not far from the long pier. Through his glasses Jonas could see Lila at the wheel and Mike's yellow parka just emerging from the forward cabin. Lila was looking this way, and when Jonas waved his jacket in the air she saw it and waved back. She pointed toward the place where Jonas's trawler was moored and turned her boat in that direction.

Jonas hurried down the porch steps to the path which led through the ferns. But he stopped and jumped up onto a driftwood log for another look through his glasses when out of the corner of his eye he noticed that the boat was changing direction again.

He couldn't see much at that distance, but Mike was apparently trying to shove Lila away from the wheel. They were obviously having an argument, and Jonas jumped down from the log to start running toward the pier. Now the boat was swinging back in that same direction but its course was erratic, and by the time Jonas reached the shore end of the pier, he could catch occasional glimpses of Lila waving her arms at Mike and he saw a yellow arm swing out to hit her.

When he scrambled up onto the weathered planks, gasping and fighting for his breath, Jonas momentarily lost sight of the boat; it was turning beneath and beyond the far end of the pier, and his running view was further blocked by one of the racing outboards which was now suspended from a crane ahead of him. He saw a Kelly grandson roll out from under the outboard and jump to his feet to look out and down toward the erratic rumbling of the sport fisherman's engine. Jonas heard a scream and checked himself to lean far over the pier railing, just in time to see the fisherman's stern swing into view, out past his trawler. Mike was hesitating, looking down toward the water. Lila was nowhere in sight. Then Mike jumped back to the wheel.

Jonas ran on again, as fast as he could. But the Kelly boy, closer and faster, was already sprinting to take a flying dive over the far railing and out of sight. Jonas heard the sport fisherman's engine roar, and as he reached the far stairway to run down to the mooring float he could see Mike desperately goosing his throttle as the boat picked up speed to move rapidly away.

Lila was floundering in the water. But then the Kelly boy reached her and together they swam safely back toward the float. Lila really needed no help, but she was so angry and frightened that she had gulped in a lot of water. And the Kelly boy was wildly excited. "He hit her," the boy yelled. "He tried to knock her down into the cabin!"

"He's out of his goddamned mind," Lila gasped, while Jonas reached to help her out of the water. "I *had* to jump! I was afraid he'd slug me again!"

"Yeah, he's crazy! The son of a bitch might have killed her!"

"Take it easy," Jonas said. "Lila, what happened?"

"Oh, why don't you ever get off your telephone?" she wailed. "I tried to reach you three times, I've been circling and going as slow as I dared—"

"Why? What were you doing over here?"

"Jonas, Mike's on something," Lila said, gasping for breath. "I'm sure he is, downers maybe. He used to do that years ago. When the pressure got too much, he'd just float away, on grass or hard stuff, whatever he could steal or buy with a phony prescription, you name it. I don't know where he found anything over there, though, unless it was in that doctor's office—"

"Over where? Stop babbling," Jonas said, wrapping his jacket around her.

"Jesus, that water's cold," the Kelly boy said. They moved toward the steps which led back up to the pier.

"Answer me, Lila. What happened?"

As she got control of herself it began to make sense. About an hour earlier, Lila had received a phone call from Mike, saying to come back over to the county seat and pick them up. It was only a short run of twenty minutes or so in the fast boat, and it never occurred to Lila that the summons didn't come from Cynthia herself, though Lila did wonder a little why they wanted to be picked up at a different landing place than they'd used before. It turned out to be a deserted fishing wharf on the edge of town and Mike was waiting there all alone. His eyes looked funny and she could tell he was scared. He made her turn around and head right back for Starfish and the hell with waiting for Cynthia Vance. Mike just wanted to grab some things at the house and pick up his car and get out of this crazy part of the country. And when Lila asked questions she began to realize that he wasn't going to let her go, he was going to make her run away with him so she couldn't tell anyone where he was. And when she tried to tell him how stupid that was, he hit her; there was just no arguing with Mike when he was full of pills or whatever it was. But fortunately, they also made him a little dizzy, and she persuaded him to lie down in the cabin to keep from getting seasick. And there were two ways to get back to Starfish from the county seat and one of them was by skirting Jonas's island, and Lila remembered that Jonas had said he'd be home and she thought maybe he could help her some way without scaring Mike more.

"What's he so afraid of, anyway?" They had reached the upper level of the pier by then; Jonas could see the sport fisherman far in the distance, running full speed on a course that would take it toward Starfish Island.

"I don't know," Lila said, "unless it's his fingerprints; they took all our fingerprints this morning. And Mike's last name isn't really Kettenring, he just borrowed that from me, years ago. So they'll find that out."

Jonas spoke quickly to the Kelly grandson. "Is there any gas in the ninety-five horse?"

"Huh?" The boy's eyes were glued to Lila's clinging wet clothes.

"The one on the boat on the crane."

"Oh, sure, it's all loaded," the boy said.

"What are you talking about?" Lila said.

"Never mind," said Jonas. "You mean Mike is just afraid they'll find out he has a record?"

"I guess so."

"For what? Murder, maybe?"

"Oh, my God, no! Jonas, he couldn't have anything

to do with anybody's murder, he's just a big stupid—"

"How about sex crimes? Is he gay?"

"No! I mean he's bi, he's whatever you want. He just does what people tell him to, that's all. But I don't know about any real heavy crimes he ever committed."

They had reached the launching crane now, and Jonas gestured to the Kelly boy. "I'm going to borrow it, okay? You take Lila up to the house, ask your grandmother to get her warm, and then stay with her, understand?"

"Don't you want me to call the cops?" the boy asked. "Sergeant Carruthers, maybe?"

"Not yet. I'll phone you."

Lila grabbed Jonas's arm. "Jonas, you're not going after him. I told you, Mike's scared and crazy—"

But Jonas was already swinging the crane out to start lowering the boat, and a couple of minutes later its big motor roared into life to smother Lila's worried objections. She wanted him to take her with him, or take the Kelly boy, or at least wait until *someone* could go with him. But Jonas couldn't hear her any more; he was already turning up the throttle and the little boat lifted in the water to go skidding away.

Desperation. That's what this whole case was about, and now he was acting just as desperately as the worst of them. But Jonas was damned if he was going to sit on his ass like Grayson wanted, not when the action was right here and now.

He could barely see the dot of white which was the sport fisherman. It was a good two or three miles ahead of him and there was no remote hope of catching up with it. But after only a few minutes Jonas could tell that at least he was gaining enough to see when the fisherman swung east of the next island. So Mike was still headed for Starfish, all right, and Jonas concentrated on getting as much speed as he dared out of the little hot-rod racer with its white geyser tail and its volcanic roar and no springs . . . oh, Lord, did it ever have no springs! Relatively calm as the sound was today, the little boat bounced like a jackhammer, except when it hit an occasional larger swell and leaped into the air to crash and throw ice water onto its already freezing pilot. Jonas was suddenly reminded of what it once felt like, as a boy, to ride an ashcan lid down an icy hard slope on Rainier, praying to God you didn't collide with a tree—and of course that reminded him, for the first time: Jesus, what if he hit one of the wayward logs left over from the storm at this speed?

But he was skidding past Shipwreck Island by then, and a short time later he rounded the southern tip of Starfish to swing in toward the big sheltered cove. He heaved a sigh of relief when he saw that the sport fisherman was there and he could finally slow down.

As he slid in beside the floating pier, however, he saw that the sport fisherman was moored only by its bowline. Mike had been in too much of a hurry to bother with the stern. So he must have realized he was being pursued. And as Jonas ran along the pier toward shore he saw that tiny ripples were lapping against the pilings which weren't from the wake he had just brought in with him. So Mike must have got here only a few minutes ago.

Jonas hurried up the ramp and through the boat shed and onto the narrow path which wound up through the salal. His hope was to reach Mike before he could leave the house in his car, if that's what Mike's plan really was. Jonas was quite sure he could handle the big ape and maybe even get some truth out of him, or at least talk some sense into him, if only he could catch up with him. It didn't occur to Jonas to worry because he didn't have a gun or any other weapon, just as it didn't occur to him to heed Lila's hysterical warnings about waiting until he could take some help along in case he needed it.

Jonas was wrong on every count. Those were all mistakes, every damn one of them. Mistakes which there just wasn't time to even realize he'd made, not in the heart-stopping split second between rounding a corner in the narrow path and catching a lightning glimpse of descending yellow close beside and behind him.

Because then there was a shock of light and a stabbing pain through his head and Jonas crashed unconscious to the ground.

22 The sky was gray, bloodshot gray, so he closed his eyes again. It was darker than the last time he had closed his eyes, but that was before he discovered this nice pillow where he could finally get some decent sleep.

"Jonas, please! Wake up!"

It was noisier than it had been the time before, too, though the voice was probably only part of his nightmare about the trees that kept crashing in the forest and the tidal waves that surged now and then inside his body. But the waves were getting smaller, even as the falling trees grew louder until they were one steady roaring ache in his head. And then he felt the shock of something cold on his face and he caught his breath. He licked his lips. They tasted metallic, like yesterday's blood. He tried his eyes again.

"Cynthia?"

"There," she cried, "now keep them open. Oh, Jonas, can't you even see me?"

She was seated on the ground and his head was apparently in her faded blue lap. She was wearing jeans and sneakers and the cold thing was a scarf soaked in icy spring water. He tried to read the designer's name which was written on the scarf.

"Of course I can," he said with great difficulty, using someone else's voice at first, "and your eyes are emerald again. But they don't match your scarf any more because it's wet."

"Oh, you idiot," she said tearfully, relievedly, as she kissed his forehead.

"Wups," he said, "careful." He rolled over to get up. Apparently it embarrassed him to be kissed by Cynthia but he didn't know why. And his sudden move only carried him as far as his hands and knees, where he braced himself against the undulating earth.

"Jonas, wait," she pleaded, "don't do that." And then, while he and the swaying moss and ferns got slowly back into rhythm, "If you feel queasy maybe you shouldn't get up at all. Because sometimes that means your skull is fractured, doesn't it? So maybe you ought to just lie there while I go call the doctor."

"My skull," Jonas said, "is very thick." And he stubbornly rose again, this time all the way to his feet.

Cynthia jumped up to support him. "Your head," she said, "is a damn mess. All I could do was get some of the dried blood off. What hit you, anyway? What happened?"

"*Who,*" he enunciated carefully, "not *what. What* was only a tree in his hand." Jonas looked around on the ground but his eyes weren't focusing yet. "Or maybe the big yellow ape just picked up the nearest rock."

Cynthia seemed shocked. "Not Mike. You don't mean Mike."

"How'd you guess?"

"I don't know. I mean, I was already thinking about Mike because his car was gone when I got home and—oh, never mind that now. I've got to get you to the hospital, if you can just walk a little."

"Wait. . . . You said *dried* blood. How long have I been here?"

"I've no idea. I just happened to look down toward the cove, and when I saw a strange boat tied up there, and saw that the sport fisherman was swinging on its mooring, I decided I'd better go down to see if something was wrong. But then here *you* were."

"I'll be damned," Jonas mumbled, finally able to see the hands of his own watch. "After five o'clock?"

"Now come on, darling, please," Cynthia said more firmly, and she started to help him up the path.

"Sure," he said. "Let's go. That's a very good idea."

While they trudged slowly upward he heard Cynthia explain that she had come home alone via the ferry and then a taxi from Shipwreck. But the driver had left her at the front door of the house, naturally, so it was almost an hour before she happened to notice that Mike's little foreign car was missing from the garage. By then Cynthia had changed her clothes and started dinner and she was getting worried about Lila, who should have been back from her shopping long before. But Cynthia couldn't imagine that Lila had taken Mike's car, or that Mike and Lila had gone anywhere together.

"You didn't notice his car when you got off the ferry?"

"No. Why would I?"

"Because that was the four o'clock ferry, wasn't it? The one that stops at Shipwreck and then heads for the mainland? I thought you might have seen Mike's car waiting to go aboard."

"No." Cynthia was both puzzled and frightened. "But of course I went straight out to the street where the taxi parks, I didn't walk through the car shed, so I wouldn't have seen him anyway. Only why would Mike be going to the mainland? Jonas, what's been happening? *Why* did he hit you?"

Jonas didn't answer. Instead, he told her where Lila was, told her that Lila was perfectly safe. Cynthia was glad to hear it, but now she seemed even more baffled than ever and rattled off more anxious questions.

Jonas still didn't answer. They had reached the top of the hill by then and the going was easier, through the meadow and the old apple orchard. Jonas's head still ached like hell, but it had cleared up enough for him to remember the urgency of those jumbled thoughts and unsolved puzzles that were still inside. The one on top burst out. "Cynthia," he said bluntly, "have they found any more of him?"

She let go of his arm and he could almost feel her face paling. "Jesus," she said after a moment, "do you have to say it that way?"

"Yes," Jonas said, "I do."

"Well, the answer is no, then. As far as I know, nobody has come running in with Trevor's left foot, or anything like that."

Jonas nodded. "That figures," he said. "They probably won't, either. After all, the main reason for chopping him up must have been so the fish would get rid of the evidence. Even the head would have disappeared if that incoming tide hadn't caught it so soon—"

"Stop it!" she almost screamed at him. "Shut up!"

Jonas was quiet. They had walked through the clump of pines by then and the open garage was ahead of them. "Sorry," he mumbled absently. But he wasn't looking at her. He was looking toward the garage.

Cynthia took a deep breath. She touched him again and spoke gently, shakily, while they moved closer to the Mercedes and the empty place beside it where Mike's little car was usually parked. "It's all right," she said. "I didn't mean to shout at you. You probably don't even know what you're saying. Now I'm going to put you in the car; it will just take me a second to run and get my keys."

Jonas pointed to a crumpled pile of yellow on the floor by the workbench. It was Mike's discarded and still-wet parka. "That's what he was wearing," Jonas said.

"Oh," she said, "yes, it's one of Trevor's old things. It was always too big for him so he let Mike wear it." She automatically reached for the parka to pick it up.

But Jonas spoke sharply. "Don't touch it. Maybe it's got some of my blood on it." He took a couple of steps into the garage to look at the place where tools were hung over the workbench. The hook where Mike had hung his machete the other day was now empty. The machete was nowhere in sight.

"Cynthia, I'd like to see Mike's room before we go. Come on."

She started to argue but obviously Jonas wasn't even hearing her yet, so she showed him Mike's room in the house as quickly as she could. There wasn't much to look at. Cynthia was startled to see that the bureau drawers were open and empty, and Mike's suitcase was gone. After Jonas stood there thinking for a minute, he let Cynthia lead him back outside, where he climbed into the Mercedes and she got in behind the wheel.

"What does it mean?" she asked nervously. "Where is Mike going?"

"I don't know," Jonas said. "Just running away, I guess."

"But why?"

"Maybe because he was mixed up in a murder?"

"If you're referring to Trevor's death," she said firmly, "Trevor was not murdered. I can't believe it. I *won't* believe it."

"All right." Jonas sighed. "Just start the car."

She did. "Yes, getting you to the doctor is all that matters now."

"No," Jonas said. "We'll stop by the ferry landing first. Reaching that four o'clock ferry would have been a pretty tight squeeze for Mike. If he didn't make it, he just might still be on Shipwreck somewhere, waiting for the seven thirty. If I could catch up with him he might have a lot of answers, whether he knows he does or not."

Cynthia opened her mouth but then shut it again and backed the car out of the garage. She turned slowly and carefully into the narrow road, which was still slippery with mud from the storm.

After a while Jonas took a deep breath and said, "Cynthia, why didn't you tell me that Mike and your husband were lovers?"

She gasped and laughed at the same time. "Because they weren't, for Christ's sake! Or if they were, *I* didn't know anything about it."

"Surely you knew about your husband's homosexuality."

"I did not. I mean, like I told Captain Grayson, it was a tendency, that's all. Just sometimes when Trevor drank too much—"

"Cynthia, stop lying."

"I'm not lying!"

"You've been lying to me ever since I met you."

"That's not true! Oh, Jonas, please, please, can't you just be quiet until after you've seen the doctor?"

"You think he'll give me a pill and make it all go away? Two murders, assault with a deadly weapon, fraud, conspiracy—"

"No! I won't listen!" she cried.

"Sure," he said, "hear no evil, see no evil. I noticed that about you, even over in Victoria."

She bit her lip. "Was that all you noticed?"

He shrugged. "Well, I did wonder why you were so anxious to see me. Unless you just wanted to stop me from what I was doing. Or wanted to keep me away from something else, that night."

She whirled to stare at him and then whirled back just in time to keep the car from sliding off the shoulder.

"You bastard," she finally whispered.

Jonas could see tears starting to cloud her eyes and he looked quickly away from her.

"I was afraid and I needed someone," she said softly. "I thought you might help me, might tell me what to do. You said we should inform the police about Trevor being missing and we did. I did everything you told me to. And by the next morning, I . . . I felt strong enough to go home again."

Jonas looked out his window and watched the wet sad trees go by. The sun would be setting soon. It was already lost behind distant fog banks. "Why didn't you ask Brig Walker for help? Don't you trust him any more?"

She hesitated for a long moment. "Maybe not," she said finally. "Maybe I've never really trusted Brig very much. But it wasn't from anything that's happened just lately, if that's what you're hinting at."

Jonas sighed. His damn head hurt. He wished they could go either faster or slower. "I'm not really sure yet what I mean, Cynthia."

She smiled. "Then why don't you just shut up and let me drive?" she said quietly.

"No," he said, even more quietly. "That's been the trouble for too many years. You've been doing too much driving. Why didn't you ever let your husband do any driving?"

Cynthia gave a startled little laugh at that. "Because Trevor drank too much, remember?"

"He didn't always," Jonas said, "not according to his wife. And I can't imagine an alcoholic spending years sailing happily all the way around the world by himself." Jonas turned to her as he went on with sudden harshness. "Cynthia, I think it's about time to turn a few things around so they make some sense. Like you made him give up sailing too, someone told me, before you'd move here to live on an island—"

"But that's different!" Cynthia interrupted. "That was because my brother had just drowned. I got over that. I wouldn't have minded, later on, only by then Trevor had simply lost his interest in sailing. Jonas, I know you don't like women who wear the pants in their families. But neither do I! For the last few years it's just been necessary, that's all."

"Oh, yes," he said, "like it was necessary for you to go all alone to haul him out of a dive, sometimes. Or necessary to keep people like me from talking to him when he was still plastered, when his tongue might be out of control—like in that alley, remember? *That's* why you drove off and left me in such a hurry."

She laughed again but he could hear shrillness in her voice, and he looked out the window once more. They were passing the turnoff to Mr. Bakewell's place. It was almost dark enough for lights to be on, but there weren't any lights visible in the cottage. Maybe Bakewell wasn't at home today.

"I don't know why you're laughing," Jonas said. "Jesus, you must have been living in panic, the way your husband was starting to come apart on you. Of course, Lila was here for the past few years and she helped keep him at home for a while, you said. And for the last six or eight months there's been Mike, who is big enough to really handle a drunk—and maybe sexy enough to do an even better job of keeping him on the reservation—"

"That's enough!" Cynthia almost shouted. "Jonas, you just admitted you're not even sure what you mean. Well, *I* certainly don't know what the hell you're talking about, so—"

"Yes, you do," he said. "And so does Mike, maybe. At least enough to make you admit a little of the truth. So let's drive a bit faster, okay?"

"Mike is nothing but a clumsy damn fool!" Cynthia said. Her face was as white as chalk and so were her fingers on the steering wheel.

"I know, that's what everybody says. But at least he must know who he's been taking orders from since Sunday. Because that's when all hell started breaking loose. Last Sunday, after a man named Wilbur Styles came here to Starfish Island. Of course, a day or two before that, Wilbur Styles had talked to your husband on the telephone and everything was sweetness and light. Wilbur reminded Trevor, on the phone, of who he was and how they had sailed together ten years ago out of San Francisco, trying out a new boat. And Trevor said yes, he remembered, and he even gave Wilbur high hopes that he might get a job out of their brief friendship in the past. Maybe he would have, too, if he'd just left it at that and waited. But Wilbur made an awful mistake. He couldn't leave things alone, he had to press. And so he came out to talk to your husband in person, face to face."

Jonas paused. Cynthia was trembling now and the car was losing its meager speed. But that was probably just as well, for they were nearing the place where the narrow road would skirt the high bluffs overlooking the dark channel between islands.

"And the reason that was such an awful mistake," Jonas said, "was because the ears can seldom remember, on a telephone, after ten years. But the eyes would remember, face to face."

"Remember what, for Christ's sake?" she whispered.

"Cynthia, I'm not just guessing. There have been all sorts of other little things. Like that romantic story you told me about your honeymooning with Trevor in the Cariboo country—and yet Lila said you weren't married until after you learned about Tre-

215

vor's inheritance, until after he gave up sailing and you agreed to come live on his island."

"So she's right!" Cynthia gasped. "Is *that* what you call lying? Is that what you're accusing me of, living in sin with Trevor for one whole summer nine years ago?"

"No," Jonas said. "But I do think you married him for purely practical reasons. So he wouldn't have to sign so many things. Or face so many people. Or put his fingerprints or signature on so many licenses or official documents or whatever. Yes, a wife could legally take over a lot of that, just like she could believably make her husband give up sailing—so he wouldn't expose his lousy, ignorant seamanship to the rest of the world."

Cynthia groaned as though she'd been hit. She was probably crying but Jonas looked only at the road. "Because the man you married," he said, "the man whom Wilbur Styles came to see and didn't recognize, the man who still tried desperately to play his part until someone ended it all with a knife or ax or machete—that man wasn't Trevor Vance at all, was he? And he wasn't just your husband. He was your brother. He was Frank Bloodworth."

They were skidding now, for her foot had automatically pushed against the brake even as she started sobbing against the steering wheel. But they only skidded a few feet before they came to a stop in the ferns beside the road. Jonas wanted to grab her and shake her hard. But he knew he wouldn't touch her, he couldn't. And then they were both startled by the sudden sharp barking of the German shepherd, which seemingly came out of nowhere to jump

216

against Cynthia's window. It wouldn't stop barking and it wouldn't stop its excited jumping, even when Cynthia turned to yell tearful commands at it. Jonas glanced back and noticed the bigger Newfoundland laboring up into view from the wooded steep slope below them. It too joined in the wild barking and jumped against the other side of the Mercedes. They were a pair of insane banshee beasts, and Cynthia started to scream.

But Jonas's eye had been caught by something else behind them, on the side of the road, and he suddenly reached to turn off the engine. He pulled out the key and jumped out of the car. He ran back along the shoulder with the dogs barking beside him but not at him until they reached a place where a car's skid marks cut through the ferns and over the edge. The German shepherd raced down out of sight, still barking and trying to lead the way.

By the time Cynthia stumbled out of her car to see what was going on, Jonas was already scrambling down through a precipitous tangle of salmonberry and alder. And then he grabbed at a tree trunk to stop himself. For there, another fifty feet farther down, caught against a clump of scraggly firs and screened from above and below by the dense undergrowth, was a small-cheap foreign car.

Jonas cautiously worked his way lower until he could see that the car lay on its side. It was Mike's car. Jonas's eyes followed the barking dog below him to see the torn-open door, the smashed glass, the man's motionless arm and blood-caked hair.

Mike was all alone and he was dead.

23

"My brother was charming and sweet, once," she said quietly. "But we had no father, and our mother died in a fire when we were in high school, and there was never enough money, even before that. I kept house and I worked nights and after I graduated I got him through school, too. Later on I even put Frank through three years of college, or I thought I did, until I learned he'd been using his last year's tuition money to set up a campus betting shop that was busted by professionals, not by the police. I found him a job in a department store but he was too smart for that, and besides he kept stealing things."

"I know," Jonas said absently, "he was charming and sweet." There were more headlights approaching the bridge from the Shipwreck side, and one of the tow trucks parked nearby was starting up its winch. Jonas moved a few steps closer to the edge of the bluff to better see the activity below and Cynthia stayed close beside him, shivering in the cold night air. The sky was almost pitch dark by now but spotlights on the tow trucks and parked sheriff's cars gave a wild, eerie glow to the scene. Cables hooked onto the wreckage of the car were starting to hoist it up toward the road. Mike's broken body had been hauled off in an ambulance almost an hour ago.

And Cynthia went stubbornly on, still trying to explain, to make everything all right. Or was she lying again to hide something else, something even worse? "Frank was all I had in the world," she said. "I was sure I could turn him into a wonderful man. But then he'd get these wild schemes. He went off with a rock group for over a year, doing publicity for their concerts. He even sent me some money, once, to buy myself a wedding present, but the man I was sleeping with turned out to be already married. Then Frank landed back on my doorstep begging for help. There was a warrant out for his arrest in Ohio, for stealing a car. The rock group had gone broke and accused him of embezzling some of their funds. A policeman's daughter claimed that Frank had raped her."

"All that and evading the draft, too." Jonas nodded. "Charming."

"Jonas, please listen. Frank wasn't just running away from the draft. There were real criminals he'd had worse trouble with. He was afraid they'd come after him. He went out to the coast, to San Diego, because he thought he might live in Mexico for a while. But then he met a man who owned a sailboat and was planning to sail it to British Columbia. Trevor Vance. And it occurred to Frank that if everyone *thought* he'd gone to Mexico, he wouldn't have any more problems if he could just disappear into Canada instead—"

"Wait a minute," Jonas said. He could see Captain

Grayson climbing up into view, moving toward one of the newly arrived cars. Jonas moved back along the road until he could see who it was that got out of the car to meet Grayson. It looked like the same doctor Jonas had seen examining Wilbur Styles's body Monday morning in the Whale Harbor hospital. Jonas wished he could hear what the doctor and Grayson were saying to each other.

"You've got to believe me," Cynthia pleaded. "Frank had nothing to do with sinking that boat off Vancouver Island. It was all just accident. Frank didn't *plan* to steal Trevor Vance's name. And *I* didn't know anything about it until I got to Tofino and there was Frank all bandaged in bed and he'd already done it! He'd been calling himself Trevor Vance for almost a week. It was already in the newspaper. Someone was already carving Frank's name on a tombstone."

"I know," Jonas said. "There's an old man over there who told me how upset you were until he assured you there'd been no foul play. I guess what you were really afraid of was that your brother might have *killed* Vance for his name."

"Maybe. I don't know what I thought, I was so shocked and scared. But mostly I was so relieved he was alive. And then I realized he was safe and he could go on being safe forever. With a brand-new identity, my mixed-up brother would finally have a chance to be the brand-new person I knew he could be."

"Sure. With a hundred thousand dollars' insurance money in his pocket."

"No! It never even occurred to me there was any insurance—"

"Not to mention an inheritance that could be parlayed into millions."

"Jonas, I didn't know about that inheritance until the lawyer came to find us."

"But your brother sure as hell must have known. He could have looked all his life and not found a better identity to steal than Trevor Vance's. A shy loner who hadn't even been seen by anyone who knew him for years and years, who spent his life sailing to far places and then wouldn't even talk about it, except maybe on a postcard to his uncle, now and then—"

"Frank found some of those postcards in a desk in the house."

"I'll bet he did! I'll bet he tore the place apart until he found some—and then quoted bits and pieces to people like Mr. Bakewell, just in case they remembered things too."

"Mr. Bakewell never suspected—I don't think he did."

"Yes, it must have really been quite easy, taking the place of a man whose only relative was a rich uncle who had just died—"

"All right! It was a horrible thing to do. Frank was horrible. I was horrible, not to have stopped it right at the beginning. But what else could I do? If I'd betrayed him, he either would have been thrown in prison or killed by gangsters! How could I know that one little lie would turn into larger and larger lies? Jonas, I didn't want money. I still don't. You've got to believe that. If there's any possible way you could get me out of this horrible mess, I'd give the island away to charity! I would! I'd do anything you say! Oh, Jonas, please listen to me. Darling, please help me . . . ?"

221

Jonas stared at her as she trailed to a stop. "Cynthia," he finally said, "I'm sorry you didn't have a father. I'm sorry Frank is dead—" He was about to say something more unkind, about his not needing a mother, but he checked himself. She looked so helpless. Was it possible she *would* do what he told her to do?

He moved abruptly away. Captain Grayson was leaving the doctor to walk up the road, and Jonas hurried to intercept him.

"Well?" Jonas said. "Have they found out how Mike died yet? What killed him?"

Grayson studied Jonas bleakly, then shrugged. "So far it's just guessing. There's a lot of lab work to be done yet, besides the full autopsy."

"But what are they guessing? I noticed Mike had a couple of bad head wounds."

Grayson sighed. "Which could have been from the blow of a blunt instrument, as in murder, or from his head smashing the steering wheel, which it did, as in accident. Since he's been dead for quite a while, they'll be equally useless on the exact time of death. Jesus, I hate doctors."

"Is that all?"

"Some slight indication of drugs. They'll do a complete analysis on that."

Jonas nodded. "They may find that Mike took a few downers."

"Is that so!" Grayson said. "Now, isn't that interesting, your having a theory like that."

"Take it easy," Jonas said quickly. "I didn't have a chance to tell you yet, that's all. Anyway, that's Lila Kettenring's guess, and if she's on her way over here now—"

"She is, with Sergeant Carruthers," Grayson said. "I just talked to him on the radio. He had to pry her loose from some Kelly kid you glued onto her this afternoon, he said. So at least she's one person who couldn't have done this. But I want *everybody* back here, damn it, and I'm getting them!"

"Yes, it's better for you to hear these things for yourself," Jonas said.

Grayson gave him a hard look, then remembered. "Oh, and you're supposed to have an X ray, the doctor says, for that bump Mike gave you. But I told him the hell with your head. Not until I'm through with it. Okay?"

"I'm all right," Jonas said. "I won't sue the county."

Grayson relaxed a bit. "Duncan," he asked, "did you know that Mike Kettenring's real name was Tate?"

"No."

"We got a report back on his prints. He had quite a record but it was mostly small-time stuff. He was a pimp once. Peddled girls and boys both."

"I'm not surprised."

"Mike also had something interesting in his car." Grayson reached into his pocket and carefully lifted out a little bundle wrapped in a handkerchief. He took his time about laying back the corners of the handkerchief until a small gun was revealed, an automatic.

"Twenty-five caliber?"

Grayson nodded. "With a serial number that's registered to your friend the Dragon Lady, up there. It's her gun that **was** stolen once, supposedly. It was in Mike's suitcase in the trunk of the car. I'm surprised you didn't find it yourself."

"I told you, I didn't touch anything here. I took Cynthia straight back to Bakewell's cottage, where we broke in and phoned you and left the dogs locked up so they couldn't touch anything either."

"All right," Grayson said, folding the gun back into his pocket. "But you see how nice and neat everything is now?"

"You mean, if that turns out to be the gun that killed Wilbur Styles."

"It will, don't worry."

"Sure," Jonas said. "So last Sunday, a man called Trevor Vance was scared by Wilbur Styles somehow and Vance told his boyfriend Mike. So Mike galloped off and shot Styles. Is that what you're thinking?"

"Exactly. But Mike was so stupid he didn't even throw the gun away. And then when Vance and Mike tangled, because of course Vance got panicky over what Mike had done, then Mike got scared too. They had a big hysterical fight, maybe, like everybody knows fairies do all the time—anyway, Mike didn't know his own strength, and when Vance was dead he chopped him up—"

"With a machete."

"Sure, maybe. And then when he realized Vance's death was being called murder, Mike decided to run away, nearly killing you in the process. But he drove too fast and his car crashed and now Mike is dead."

"And now it's all over."

"That's right."

"Two stupid murders by a big stupid ape who then died in an accident."

"Check. Case closed. We can all go home now." Grayson stared at Jonas for a long moment before he sighed. "Only you don't believe one more fucking word of that than I do."

"No," Jonas said thoughtfully, "but that gun being found in Mike's suitcase just might help confirm something we both probably *do* believe."

"Such as?"

"That there were really three murders, and the gun was planted there by the murderer. That Mike was really killed this afternoon and then his car was pushed over the edge. Pushed by the same person who had killed Styles last Sunday and had kept the gun so it could be planted in a good place if necessary. And today that became necessary. Because this same desperate person also murdered the man you call Trevor Vance—and Mike probably knew it, or guessed it, and Mike was beginning to panic; so the killer decided to eliminate him too, laying all the blame on him at the same time." Jonas paused for a moment. "That's about it, I'd say."

Grayson nodded slowly. "You said some very interesting things there, Duncan. Only you said a little more than I expected." Grayson gestured toward Cynthia, who still stood farther up the road where Jonas had left her. "What's the lady been telling you, anyway? Let's hear it. What the hell have you two been talking about?"

"This and that," Jonas shrugged. "Ancient history, mostly."

"Now look, Duncan—"

"It can wait," Jonas said sharply. "What you need is some proof of murder in a hurry, or you *will* have a closed case on your hands. Is Mr. Bakewell in that last car that drove in, down there?"

"What? No, that's Brighton Walker and his boy Terrence Fall you wanted to see. Bakewell's over in Bellingham, but the old man doesn't really know anything. He's just been visiting his sister until he can get his own television fixed."

"All right, what about tracks? Have your boys finished checking the road yet?"

"As much as they can, at night. But there's been rain off and on. Tracks won't prove who might have been here during a limited time period, like this afternoon when Mike's car went over the edge there."

Jonas looked up toward Cynthia, who stood shivering and alone. She still hadn't told him all of the truth. Would she be willing to help him? He looked down toward the car, where Brig Walker apparently preferred to remain rather than comfort her. "Captain," Jonas said, "you worry too much about reality. It's desperation I care about. Suppose I could make it work for us instead of against us, so we *would* have some evidence."

"Whose desperation? Who is it, Duncan? Who are you gunning for?"

"Will you give me an hour to see if I'm right?"

24 Somewhere in the wet darkness overhead he heard the soft cry of a great horned owl. It was answered by another owl, and Jonas no longer wondered at the absolute silence in the ferny woods beside the dark road. This was a time for prudent small creatures to huddle in their bramble thickets or warm beds of grass. Which was exactly where he ought to be himself, Jonas thought. His head hurt and his eyes hurt and his right shin hurt where he'd banged into a storm-fallen branch in the darkness. The little two-cell flashlight he'd borrowed from Grayson needed new batteries, just as it was supposed to.

The owl hooted again, louder this time, and there was a splash of steps hurrying closer, accompanied by the waving yellow glow of an even more useless flashlight. "Hey, what's that?" whispered Terrence Fall.

"Just an owl," Jonas said. "Any luck?"

"Hell, no." The young man sounded very nervous. "Just a few of those same tracks of the Mercedes is all. I don't know what we're doing out here, anyway."

"I thought you might be willing to help me. Those deputies didn't look very hard; they never do."

Terrence banged his flashlight against his leg. For a second it glowed brighter but then it faded to the color of dying candlelight. "No wonder," Terrence said, "if this is the kind of junk the county equips them with."

"Mine will still last for a while," Jonas said. "Come on, let's work back the other way again, back toward Shipwreck."

"Couldn't we just go on to the house, to get warm for a while? I mean, that's three times we've been along this same stretch."

"I need your help, Terrence. You've got better eyes than I have."

"Well, that's what I mean, sir! That bandage on your head looks pretty awful. Maybe you ought to be lying down or something."

The young man sounded really concerned about him. So had Cynthia, earlier. So did Lila, when they brought her over from Whale Harbor and she heard what had happened. So did Brig Walker, probably, though Walker obviously didn't want to commit himself on anything right now.

"Why do they want to see everybody?" Terrence asked. "What's going on down there at the house?"

Jonas shrugged. "Captain Grayson is getting statements on where everybody has been today, that's all. It's routine in a murder case. He's probably working over your boss, right now. Walker went out somewhere in his plane this afternoon, I understand, after he left his lawyers."

"Yeah, he wanted to look at some real estate is what he said." Even in the darkness Terrence looked worried. "But listen, none of those deputies said anything about Mike being *murdered*. I mean, it's not surprising if he just skidded over the edge back there, the way he drove that little piece of tin sometimes. He even tried to run me off the road once and thought it was a big joke."

"When you were on your motorcycle, you mean?" Jonas stopped to aim his flashlight at an angle along the ground. "Here," he said, "here, this is what I've been looking for."

Terrence stooped to peer at the place Jonas gestured to. "What's that supposed to be?"

"Something I noticed when we drove along here earlier. Aren't those diamond-shaped marks made by the tires on your Harley?"

"I guess they might be. But those tracks are about a week old, I'd say. Wouldn't you?"

"Maybe." Jonas sighed, standing up, looking around again. "It seemed to me the spot I saw looked fresher than that." He shook his head and moved on again, waving the weak beam of his flashlight back and forth along the shoulder of the road.

Terrence's flashlight flickered and died for good, but Terrence didn't even notice. "Well, I do come out here quite a lot, Mr. Duncan. Just running errands for Mr. Walker usually, that's all."

"Like today, maybe? Were you out here today?"

"Of course not!" Terrence's quick laugh was almost too quick and much too loud.

Jonas glanced at his watch. They would be reaching the turnoff to Mr. Bakewell's cottage soon. He walked closer to Terrence and spoke gently. "Son, I noticed once before that you're not a very good liar."

"I'm not lying! What is this, anyway? Did somebody say I was out here? Did somebody see me here, is that what you're getting at?"

"Take it easy," Jonas said. "I'm sure if you were here there's a perfectly simple explanation."

"Christ, yes! I mean, I never had any trouble with Mike. I never had any trouble with anybody! Only I *wasn't* here, so . . ."

He stopped as Jonas dropped to his knees beside a mud puddle to peer closely at more tracks. "There. Maybe this is the place that caught my eye. Yes, this looks a lot fresher."

Terrence licked his lips. "If you say so. Only it's been raining off and on so many times. . . ."

"I know, and on a one-track road like this each track smears the last one. But with a bike you can hit the shoulder sometimes—"

Terrence interrupted him with another sudden laugh. "Hey, this was probably made day before yesterday! Sure, I was out here for a few minutes day before yesterday."

Jonas stood up. He shook his head. "Don't try so hard, son. That's the first secret of good lying."

"Oh, for Christ's sake—"

"And don't protest so much. Who is it you're trying to protect, just yourself? *Were* you out here today? You usually do come out on Saturdays, I understand."

"I don't know what you're talking about!"

Jonas still spoke quietly. "Yes, you do. And I think you're scared to death and I don't blame you. Because you could be next on the list, you know."

"What?"

"Mike followed orders and now he's dead. Mike was dumb, he was a sucker." Jonas touched the boy's arm. "But there's no reason for you to be one. Or to be dumb or dead, either. Terrence, I know what must have happened today, it's the only way everything ties together. So trust me, will you? I'm not a cop. You can tell me whatever it is you've done. I'm not going to pick on you for it."

The young man pulled away from him, almost hysterically. "No! I haven't done anything, God damn it! I'm going up to the house. I won't listen to any more of this shit!"

He turned to walk away but Jonas jumped after him. Jonas had already spotted a rock on the ground and he took aim at it as he called "Wait!" and pretended to trip and then fell heavily to the ground. His flashlight smashed against the rock. He roared with quite real pain in his head from the shock of the fall. He threw the now-useless flashlight aside. In the darkness he could vaguely see Terrence hurrying back to kneel anxiously beside him.

"Mr. Duncan!" the boy cried, "are you all right? Oh, damn it, you shouldn't even be out here like this!"

Terrence actually sounded scared to death about him, so Jonas just lay there for a moment, getting some breath back into his tired lungs, groaning a bit. There was a faint rustle of movement from the nearby path to Bakewell's cottage. Terrence whirled, listening. Jonas chuckled weakly. "Guess I even scared the rabbits." He started to rise and Terrence tried to help him but Jonas brushed him off. "No, no, I can manage." And in a loud, firm voice he said, "You go on along to the house, now. I'll just walk back over the hill; it's a lot closer and there are still

231

a couple of deputies on duty there. They'll help me. I'll be all right."

"Okay, sure," Terrence said relievedly and he turned to move off again. There was another rustle of movement in the thick dark undergrowth, and he veered nervously toward the middle of the road.

"And thanks, Terrence," Jonas suddenly called after him in his loudest voice. "You've been a big help to me! I won't give you away. I'll do what I can to protect you, don't worry!"

Thirty or forty feet along the road now, Terrence whirled. What the hell was *that* all about? "Mr. Duncan?" But Jonas had disappeared; he was nowhere in sight. Terrence swore shakily to himself—and then caught his breath and felt a cold chill in his back as he heard the soft sound of a small chain from one side and not far away.

Jonas, who had ducked off the road farther on, heard the chain sound too. He moved silently, rapidly, back through the trees until he could see a dark form bending over two large dark objects—the two dogs. The person bending over them could obviously handle them well, for both dogs were completely silent and almost motionless. But then there was another soft chain sound and the dark figure straightened up. With their leashes slipped from their chain collars, the dogs raced up onto the road.

Terrence was already starting to run when he heard the first roar from the huge Newfoundland. He glanced back to catch a vague glimpse of the lighter-colored German shepherd racing toward him. He yelled in fright and then in desperation as he dived to one side toward a tree and spun around with his back to it to kick at the charging dogs. They leaped and barked but they were growling at their some-time tormentor, too, and Terrence grabbed up a stick to swing at them.

It was then that he saw a shadowy, lithe figure jump up onto the road and run gracefully closer be-hind the dogs. It was a woman, and in her hands was Bakewell's shotgun.

Jonas, meantime, still kept out of sight as he ran closer through the trees. He could hear the leaping dogs getting more and more excited, and then Ter-rence's voice yelling, "Get them off! Damn it, get them off! What's the matter with you?"

Jonas jumped up onto the road just in time to see, in dark silhouette, that the woman had stopped and was slowly raising her shotgun, even as Terrence started to scream.

"Christ, put that thing down!" the boy cried. "I didn't tell him anything! I didn't tell anybody! They can't prove I was here! Put it down! Are you crazy? Don't! Lila, please! *Lila!*"

And then Terrence collapsed as he saw Jonas qui-etly take the gun from the woman's trembling hands. She was staring at Terrence in horror.

"Thanks, Cynthia," Jonas said. "Thanks for help-ing. You'd better get the dogs off him now."

25

"... and I'm sorry I hit Mr. Duncan so hard with that rock, down there in the salal. I didn't mean to, but I was scared shitless. I could see this little boat catching up with me, and then there was Duncan running up the path after me, and I knew I could never get away from the house without his seeing me, or at least he'd hear my motorcycle starting up and know it had been me instead of Mike in the yellow parka—"

"You can go slower if you like, son," a plainclothes-man said quietly. "We have plenty of time. It was you, not Mike, in the yellow parka on the boat today; pick it up from there. Lila Kettenring made you wear the parka—"

"But she didn't *make* me do anything! Don't you understand? When I came out here, early this afternoon, and found Lila waiting for me on the road all upset, it just never occurred to me she wasn't telling the truth. She'd heard this awful crash, she said, and discovered that Mike had had an accident in his car. Well, after everything that had been going on—and everybody knows that Mike and Lila fought all the time—I just wanted to help her any way I could! I

234

mean, to keep her from getting in trouble for something that wasn't her fault! *I* knew she hadn't caused that accident or killed Mike or anything like that . . . or I thought I did . . . or Christ, maybe I didn't even stop to think, I don't know. . . ."

Terrence's pleading voice sounded painfully naked, like the fluorescent lights in the next room which jarred Jonas's eyes as he moved away from the droning confession. Desperation, he thought. It's contagious. But so is sex, and the boy obviously would have done anything Lila had asked of him. Jonas didn't need to hear any more. Lila probably thought she'd been very clever in the way she'd grabbed the opportunity to set herself up with a perfect alibi, using Terrence's handy Saturday visit and Jonas's neighborly nearness to make it seem that Mike was still alive. Surely Mike's body wouldn't be discovered for some time, so the discrepancy in the time of his death would never be caught. And Lila's stories to Jonas had been convincing. She had even thought to cover the possible discovery of drugs in Mike's stomach, the downers which she had no doubt fed him herself so she could manage the big ape when she killed him. After that, her act with Terrence in the boat was dangerous and exciting; she probably thought it was fun. Maybe Lila even got orgasms out of danger sometimes. Jonas saw that she was over by the boat models now, happily explaining their rigging to two deputies who were supposed to be guarding and watching her. They were watching her body particularly well, Jonas noticed.

Oh, the hell with Lila. Jonas could feel his head aching worse in this big room where some people

235

looked like cadavers and others looked like man-
nequins onstage in a glamorous setting of display
boards filled with the good life, the rich life, the dead
life. Cynthia sat frozen in a chair to one side, watching Lila incredulously and whispering to Grayson,
who took notes and looked shocked. Grayson saw
Jonas and moved over to join him.

"Jesus," Grayson muttered. "You sure triggered
something."

Jonas sighed. "I guess it's not easy to live with guilt
year after year, even for the most experienced, the
most guilty."

"Well, Mrs. Vance, or whatever we call her now,
she was just telling me—"

"I was thinking about her brother. How he finally
began to show the pressure, three years ago. That's
when his drinking started getting out of control. I
noticed that quite a few things dated from then."

"From the time when Lila came here."

Jonas nodded. "An airlines hostess who met them
by accident—and pretty quick began to own them."

Grayson grinned ruefully. "And I kept thinking
Wilbur Styles was somehow a blackmailer!"

"I told you that didn't make any sense. How could
Styles risk it, a three-time loser on parole? One whiff
of attempted extortion—"

"I know. Back in the clink forever."

"Besides, he wanted to see me. We know he was
scared to death. He must have been desperate for
help and advice about something that was too big
and too dangerous for him to handle. But that
couldn't have been just his recognizing that Frank
Bloodworth was an imposter. Styles wouldn't have

been that afraid of Frank, or vice versa; under all the circumstances, Frank probably could have bought him off with a nickel. But then I suddenly realized: what Styles must have known was that someone *else* here on Starfish had recognized *him* from the past. And the most dangerous person that could be would be a *real* blackmailer into whose territory he had obviously intruded!"

"Her. Lila. And since she was about the only other person here that day—"

"It wasn't that simple; people could have lied about where they were." Jonas cleared his throat and spoke louder as he strolled closer to the model table where Lila held her oblivious court. "But I did remember something that happened, the other day, here in this same room. Frank Bloodworth almost lost his control, he almost came apart right in front of me. But then Lila snapped on those awful lights. So I should have guessed the truth about her right then, the way she always hovered, the quick way she reminded him to shut up."

"You've done good enough with the guesses. I won't complain."

Jonas ignored that. "So then I asked him my last question, about the favor Styles claimed he'd once done for Vance. He answered with a crazy crack about how maybe Styles had once got him a price on a case of tequila or saved him from a social disease by chasing some chippy away from his boat—and then Lila *really* shut him up and I had to leave."

He paused. Grayson was looking at Lila, too. Her fingers still danced along the rigging of the sloop in demonstration of something, but her words to the deputies were only occasional whispers. At least a part of her was listening.

"Anyway, that story of chasing a girl away was a little like something Dora Styles had told me Wilbur once did," Jonas continued. "It was one of the things Wilbur bragged about, or joked about. He claimed he'd once scared a lovelorn girl off a friend's back by serving phony child-support claims made by the friend's two nonexistent wives. . . ." Jonas stopped as he noticed that Lila's fingers on the sloop's rigging stopped moving for a split second and then fluttered even faster than before.

"Lousy trick," Grayson said, "even to pull on a chippy."

She didn't hear it. She was laughing and chattering to the deputies once more.

"The favor Styles had done for the real Trevor Vance," Jonas said, speaking softly as they strolled on, satisfied by what he had seen. "It must have been something like that. Maybe she really loved Trevor Vance."

"And then years later she runs into a guy and his wife on a plane who were wearing Vance's name, living on Vance's island—what a setup for a shakedown!"

"That's right. And the deeper Cynthia and Frank got into their development deals, the bigger Lila's final payoff would have been. She knew it and they knew it, and what could they do about it? No wonder Lila was so quick to kill Styles, to keep him from telling anyone what he knew. And when Frank Bloodworth panicked and drank and showed signs of breaking, Lila simply got rid of him, too. No one would have ever suspected he hadn't just gone off drunk in his boat and died in the storm, disappeared forever. And then this whole place would have belonged to Cynthia, who was already so involved with guilt that she'd go on paying blackmail for ever and ever."

"Yeah," Grayson said. "Only you look like you've got a fever, you know that?"

"Sure," said Jonas, "I know that. It's this place gives me one. But wait. Next came Mike. Because after the fish failed to eat that head, Lila had to change her plan. Well, six or eight months ago I think Lila got Mike here on purpose. She was discovering she couldn't handle Frank Bloodworth any more, to keep him in line, and neither could Cynthia. So Lila got her bi husband from the past to come and help, to keep the phony Vance a little happier. Only now, when all hell broke loose—you see what I mean?"

"Of course. We already figured that out."

"Stupid as he was, Mike would have guessed awfully fast that Bloodworth was maybe hacked up on the fish-cleaning board of the sport fisherman. So Lila decided to lay everything off on Mike, and today—"

"All right!" Grayson said firmly. "But now Sergeant Carruthers is going to take you out for that X ray, okay?"

Jonas took a deep breath. He didn't feel dizzy. It was just this place, that's all.

"Grayson," he said, "do you know that a starfish can extrude its stomach?"

"Huh?"

"It can just work its way into the shells of mussels and clams and stay there until there's nothing left but empty shells. . . ."

Jonas stopped. Bill Carruthers was taking hold of

his arm now, and Jonas finally nodded to Grayson. Together he and Bill started to walk out.

Cynthia was watching. She jumped anxiously up out of her chair and pushed a deputy aside to hurry closer.

"Jonas? You're not going!" she said.

"I'm sorry," he said quickly, gently. "But I only told you I'd do what I can. Well, I've done it. That's it."

240